P9-DXT-213

Time passed slowly as Sam watched Wade—more specifically as she ogled his chest.

For a guy who wore a suit to work he had nicely defined pecs and biceps. Not the bulging muscles the cowboys flaunted but the lean, hard muscles of a swimmer or a runner. Sam studied the intriguing patch of dark hair in the middle of his chest, before following it down his stomach, where it disappeared beneath the waistband of his jeans. When her eyes reversed direction, she discovered Wade staring at her.

Their gazes clashed and Wade's brown eyes smoldered with invitation.

Oh, boy. She was in trouble.

Big trouble.

Dear Reader,

Everyone is forgetful at times, but Samantha Cartwright's forgetfulness comes from an injury that almost took her life as a teenager. She's convinced her handicap stands in the way of what she really wants—a family of her own.

I created Wade Dawson to rescue Samantha, but he isn't your typical cowboy. As a matter of fact, he's the furthest thing from a cowboy—he's a financial adviser. But Wade shows Samantha that it's not the clothes that make a man a cowboy—it's pure stubborn determination. And Wade has plenty of that.

I hope you enjoy watching Samantha and Wade fall in love. If you missed my books about Samantha's brothers Duke (*The Cowboy and the Angel*, Nov 2008) and Matt (*A Cowboy's Promise*, April 2009), both books remain available through online retailers or may be ordered by your local bookstore. Late in 2010 be on the lookout for a fourth sibling, who mysteriously resurfaces to claim his rightful place in the Cartwright family.

For more information on my books visit www.marinthomas.com. For up-to-date news on Harlequin American Romance authors and their books visit www.harauthors.blogspot.com.

Happy reading!

Marin

Samantha's Cowboy

MARIN THOMAS

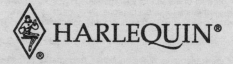

TORONTO • NEW YORK • LONDON
AMSTERDAM • PARIS • SYDNEY • HAMBURG
STOCKHOLM • ATHENS • TOKYO • MILAN • MADRID
PRAGUE • WARSAW • BUDAPEST • AUCKLAND

If you purchased this book without a cover you should be aware
that this book is stolen property. It was reported as "unsold and
destroyed" to the publisher, and neither the author nor the
publisher has received any payment for this "stripped book."

Recycling programs
for this product may
not exist in your area.

ISBN-13: 978-0-373-75275-1

SAMANTHA'S COWBOY

Copyright © 2009 by Brenda Smith-Beagley.

All rights reserved. Except for use in any review, the reproduction or
utilization of this work in whole or in part in any form by any electronic,
mechanical or other means, now known or hereafter invented, including
xerography, photocopying and recording, or in any information storage
or retrieval system, is forbidden without the written permission of the
publisher, Harlequin Enterprises Limited, 225 Duncan Mill Road,
Don Mills, Ontario M3B 3K9, Canada.

This is a work of fiction. Names, characters, places and incidents are
either the product of the author's imagination or are used fictitiously,
and any resemblance to actual persons, living or dead, business
establishments, events or locales is entirely coincidental.

This edition published by arrangement with Harlequin Books S.A.

® and TM are trademarks of the publisher. Trademarks indicated with
® are registered in the United States Patent and Trademark Office, the
Canadian Trade Marks Office and in other countries.

www.eHarlequin.com

Printed in U.S.A.

ABOUT THE AUTHOR

Marin Thomas grew up in Janesville, Wisconsin. She attended the University of Arizona in Tucson on a Division I basketball scholarship. In 1986 she graduated with a B.A. in radio-television and married her college sweetheart in a five-minute ceremony in Las Vegas. Marin was inducted in May 2005 into the Janesville Sports Hall of Fame for her basketball accomplishments. Even though she now calls Chicago home, she's a living testament to the old adage "You can take the girl out of the small town, but you can't take the small town out of the girl." Marin's heart still lies in small-town life, which she loves to write about in her books.

Books by Marin Thomas

Don't miss any of our special offers. Write to us at the following address for information on our newest releases.

Harlequin Reader Service
U.S.: 3010 Walden Ave., P.O. Box 1325, Buffalo, NY 14269
Canadian: P.O. Box 609, Fort Erie, Ont. L2A 5X3

To my niece Desirée—
because you never gave up.
As you look to a future full of possibilities
always remember…

*The best helping hand that you will ever receive
is the one at the end of your own arm.*
—Fred Dehner

Chapter One

Samantha Cartwright was fit to be boiled down to glue—that said a lot for a woman who intended to run a sanctuary ranch for neglected horses.

She swung her Chevy Silverado pickup into the no-parking zone in front of First Place Tower at 15 East Fifth Avenue in downtown Tulsa, Oklahoma. Three o'clock on a Friday afternoon and not a soul in sight. The mid-July hundred-degree heat wave had sent the city's business professionals home early.

Charles Dawson's ornery backside better be in his office.

No sooner had Sam's dusty Ropers hit the pavement than a security guard materialized out of thin air. Sucking in his baby smooth cheeks, he pointed to the sign at the curb. Sam fumbled with the floor mat until her fingers found the fifty-dollar bill she kept hidden for emergencies—empty gas tanks or bribes.

"The…sign…says…No…Parking." The young man emphasized each word as if Sam was slow on the uptake.

She willed herself not to react to the insult. He

couldn't know that her *uptake* was indeed problematic at times. "I'm not parking here." She slapped the keys and the money into his palm. "You're taking my truck for a spin around the block until I return."

His cheeks inflated like air bags, as he protested, "Ma'am, I can't." But she noticed his fingers curled around the cash.

"Of course you can—" Sam read the name embroidered on the front of his blue uniform "—Dave." She strode toward the building's entrance, catching her reflection in the dark glass doors. She should have showered and changed into street clothes before driving into the city. Oh, well. Sam had ceased trying to impress men years ago. No matter how she dolled herself up or how many male heads she turned, in the end her shortcomings sent them running. Not even the Cartwright name had been enough to coax a down-on-his-luck cowboy to stick by her side.

"May I help you?" A woman in a lilac-colored suit with blond hair neatly tucked at the nape of her neck stood behind a crescent-shaped kiosk in the middle of the lobby.

Now that Sam had sacrificed the time to make the hour drive into Tulsa everyone appeared eager to assist her—except Mr. Dawson who hadn't had the courtesy to return one of the several messages she'd left for him over the past two weeks.

The purple flower flashed a placating smile as her French-manicured thumbnail clicked and unclicked the ballpoint pen in her hand. Sam approached the desk, forcing the petite blonde to crane her neck to maintain eye contact. At five feet nine inches, Sam towered over most women.

"Thanks, but I'm afraid the only person able to help me is Mr. Dawson." Sam veered toward the bank of elevators at the back of the lobby, her boot heels clacking against the marble floor. A plaque on the wall indicated Dawson Investments occupied the fourteenth floor. According to the directory, the building did not have a thirteenth floor.

Once inside the elevator, she patted the front of her jeans, double-checking that the note she'd written earlier in the morning remained tucked inside the pocket. *Stick to your agenda and all will be fine.*

The doors opened to another lobby and another blond receptionist—this one wearing a fuchsia-colored suit. The woman gave Samantha a head-to-toe glance, nose curling with disgust. "Good afternoon."

"I'm here to see Charles Dawson."

"Did you have an appointment with Mr. Dawson?" The receptionist flipped furiously through the day planner on the desk. "I'm positive I rescheduled all of his commitments."

"This is a spur-of-the-moment visit."

Veronica Smith—according to the nameplate on the desk—blew out a breath and pressed a hand to her heart. "Oh, good. I didn't make a mistake." Her smile widened. "I'm sorry, but Mr. Dawson is out of town."

Blast it! "When will he return?"

"Not for a few weeks. He's overseas combining pleasure with business."

Sam would've loved to have given Mr. Dawson the pleasure of her boot against his backside. "Who's covering for Mr. Dawson in his absence?"

"His nephew, Wade, I mean Mr. Dawson, is handling things."

"Fine. I'll see Wayne then."

"Wade. Wade with a *D*."

Whatever. Sam's nerves pulled taut. "I need to speak with him right away."

"Mr. Dawson is in a meeting."

She'd been pushed to the end of her rope and now someone was going to hang. "I'm not leaving until I see Mr. Wade-with-a-*D* Dawson."

Veronica frowned. "Excuse me, but who are you?"

"Samantha Cartwright." In case the woman was totally clueless, she added, "Cartwright Oil."

The blonde's eyes rounded, then she tapped her pencil against the desk calendar. "Let me see if I can squeeze you in…"

Sam hadn't driven sixty-five miles to be squeezed in anywhere. Each time she'd phoned Dawson Investments one of the secretaries had reassured her that her call would be returned. At first Samantha had second-guessed herself and worried that she'd forgotten to leave a message or worse—she'd thought she'd called but hadn't. After one week she'd kept a log of her phone calls to the firm.

Enough was enough. She left Veronica flipping the pages of her day planner and strolled through the office doors of Dawson Investments. *Where to find…Wade with a* D?

She marched down a corridor of glassed-in conference rooms. *Bingo.* At the end of the hall several men in monkey suits crowded around an oval table. The man seated at the head of the table with his back to Sam read a document out loud. The other apes appeared bored to death—one twirled his pencil on his palm. Another played with his BlackBerry. Four others stared bug-eyed into space. And the chimpanzee nearest to her sketched cartoon figures in the margins of a memo.

Sam rapped her knuckles against the glass pane.

The pencil twirler knocked his coffee into his lap. The artist scrambled to cover his drawings. And one of the men who'd been zoning out toppled backward in his chair and landed on the floor, staring at the ceiling.

She'd take a brooding cowboy any day over these pansies in suits.

Finally the head pansy shifted in his seat and stared at her through black-rimmed glasses. Hair neatly styled, no sign of a five o'clock shadow and unlike the other men in the room, he wore a pocket protector in his crisp white shirt along with the traditional red power tie—knot perfectly done.

Mr. Wade with a *D* was a nerd, albeit a handsome nerd.

His dark brown eyes pinned her and the air rushed from her lungs leaving her light-headed. He waved her into the room.

She didn't need to be asked twice.

"May I help you?" The rumble of his deep voice contradicted his clean-shaven nerdiness. In her opinion his voice was better suited for whispering sweet nothings behind the barn than translating company performance reports. The outer corner of one dark eyebrow rose above his black frames. *Shoot.* What had he asked?

"Gentlemen, we'll resume this meeting on Monday. Enjoy an early start to your weekend."

The monkeys gathered their belongings and disappeared. Once the door closed, Sam exhaled a sigh of relief. Crowds made her nervous and she appreciated Wade with a *D*'s thoughtfulness in clearing the room.

Left alone with Calamity Jane, Wade studied the daughter of oil tycoon Dominick Cartwright. Sixteen years had passed since he'd last seen her. Time had transformed a pretty teenage girl into a breathtaking woman. Not even dirt-smudged cheeks, a messy ponytail or faded jeans and a wrinkled shirt detracted from her beauty. Evidence of Spanish ancestry, which rumor claimed she'd inherited from her mother, was apparent in her dusky skin, pitch-black hair, high cheekbones and almond-shaped dark eyes. He hadn't remembered her being this tall—standing almost eye-to-eye with him—and he resisted rolling forward onto the balls of his feet to gain another inch.

Samantha's gaze circled the room, skipping over him. Where was the smart-mouthed, self-confident braggart who'd once called him a wimp because he couldn't climb a tree? He held out his hand. Her grip was warm, firm and callused, her fingernails bitten down to the quick—not the hands of a pampered princess. "Nice to see you again, Samantha."

A wrinkle formed in the middle of her forehead. "Have we met before?"

The question shot through his ego like a marksman's arrow. Apparently he hadn't made much of an impression on her all those years ago—par for the course. He wasn't a man women swooned over. Even his ex-wife had labeled him and their marriage *unremarkable.*

"Uncle Charles and your father were college buddies at the University of Oklahoma." When that didn't jar her memory, he added, "I accompanied my uncle to the

Lazy River Ranch years ago." Wade had been a junior in college, majoring in finance, when his uncle had suggested he meet one of Dawson Investment's biggest clients. At the time Wade had no idea his uncle intended to put him in charge of managing Samantha's trust fund once Wade had joined the firm two years later. "You offered me a lesson in tree climbing that afternoon." After an uncomfortable silence, Wade accepted that Samantha didn't remember him.

Feeling like an idiot, he motioned her to the nearest chair. She remained standing and he swallowed his irritation. "What can I do for you?"

"I've phoned the office several times, but my messages have gone unreturned. Not until today did I learn that your uncle was out of town on business."

Darn Veronica. The receptionist his uncle had hired was an airhead. "I apologize for the inconvenience."

"You should. Better yet, you might have had the courtesy to at least return one of my calls, seeing how my father's money keeps this firm afloat."

Now this was the Samantha Cartwright he remembered—bossy and arrogant. Oddly, her waspish attitude put him at ease—much better than the damsel-in-distress expression she'd worn moments ago. He'd never considered himself hero material and no female had ever asked him to save her. "Please accept my apologies. How may I assist you?"

Instead of launching into a tirade, Samantha patted her clothes. Wade found it impossible not to follow the path of her hand, especially when she pressed her fingers against her breast before they dropped to her jeans where she removed a slip of paper from the pocket. She scanned the note, then announced, "I'd like to cash in my trust fund."

Since joining his uncle's firm Wade had worked diligently to grow Samantha's savings. As a matter of fact he'd increased her net worth by several million dollars. "How old are you?"

"Thirty-two. As of today."

She was of legal age to withdraw money from the trust without her father's consent. Wade was positive he hadn't received a reminder of Samantha's upcoming birthday from the e-mail system he'd set up to notify him of changes in the status of client accounts.

"Are you going to stand there and ogle me or do I get my money?"

Wade would have preferred to ogle but said, "Let's continue this discussion in my office." He held open the door and when she brushed past him, he caught a whiff of honeysuckle—the delicate feminine scent at odds with the sullied, sharp-tongued cowgirl. Wade's office was a windowless room in the middle of the floor—but not for long. He was in line for a promotion to vice president and the position came with a corner office and a view of downtown Tulsa.

"Something to drink? Water? Coffee?" he asked, as soon as Samantha claimed the chair in front of his desk.

"No, thank you."

Wade wiggled his computer mouse until the screen saver popped up—a photograph of his eight-year-old son, Luke, proudly displaying his first-place spelling-bee ribbon. A few typed passwords later and Wade had Samantha's personal information in front of him.

Yes, indeed. Samantha Cartwright was thirty-two

years old today. For the life of him, Wade couldn't figure out why she was dressed like a ranch hand on her birthday. He'd have expected her to spend the day getting dolled up for a celebratory night on the town. "Happy birthday," he said.

"It will be once I have my money."

What did a pampered rich girl want with millions of dollars? Last he'd heard she worked in her father's company pulling down a substantial salary—probably doing nothing but sitting at a desk and looking beautiful—like Veronica.

Before Wade accessed the financial particulars of her account, he asked, "Is your father aware that you intend to withdraw money from your trust?"

Her chin jutted. "No, and I'd rather he wasn't contacted."

The hair on the back of Wade's neck stood on end. As his son would say…Wade smelled a stinker. He suspected Samantha was up to no good, but just how far did he stick his nose into her business without crossing the line? "What are your plans for the money?" He'd worked his ass off researching and selecting investments guaranteed to increase the wealth of her holdings. He hated to see his hard work squandered on a Paris Hilton-type shopping spree.

"Am I required to tell you in order to receive my money?"

"No," he answered honestly.

Her attention shifted to the filing cabinet in the corner, then the keyboard, then the desk calendar before making eye contact with him. "I'm opening a sanctuary ranch for abandoned and neglected horses."

Now red flags flapped inside Wade's head. What did a wealthy woman want with rescuing horses? He suspected Samantha's ranch was nothing more than a pet project she'd ditch once boredom set in.

"I purchased an old farmstead and I need the money to make several renovations." Her fingers crushed the yellow notepaper in her hand.

"As your financial adviser I'm obligated to warn you that a horse sanctuary isn't a sound investment." An image of a stallion eating from a feed bin filled with hundred-dollar bills popped into his head.

Her eyes narrowed. "The ranch may not be a money-making venture, but saving horses is a noble cause."

Wade wasn't a horse lover. The private school he'd attended before college boasted riding stables, but after landing in the dirt several times during his first and only riding lesson, Wade had participated in indoor activities such as debate and math club. He had to talk sense into Samantha before she wasted years of his time and effort.

Legally he was required to hand over her money no matter how foolish her plans, yet he had a responsibility to Dawson Investments to dispense client funds in a manner that least impacted the company's bottom line.

"What amount do you need to get this project off the ground?" he asked.

"I hadn't considered…" She waved her hand in the air. "I'm positive the funds in my account will be more than enough to cover the costs."

Heartburn stung Wade's chest. He had a hunch Samantha had jumped into this venture without creating a budget. "My suggestion would be to withdraw money in smaller increments, allowing the remainder of your funds to continue earning interest." That was sound advice and Dawson Investments would then be able to absorb the loss at a slower pace. "Have you made a list of property improvements?"

She uncrumpled the note in her fist. He caught a glimpse of the chicken scratch on the paper but couldn't make out the words. "I need to dig a well."

She bought a ranch with no water source?

"The previous owner's well is almost dried up," she continued.

"Have you contacted a water-drilling company?"

"No—"

Samantha Cartwright hadn't a lick of sense. She should have paid a drilling company to confirm that there was water in the ground before she'd purchased the homestead.

"—but Millicent assures me there's water."

"Who's Millicent?"

"A water witch who lives on the property."

You've got to be kidding. Avoiding the topic of water witches all together, he asked, "What other repairs and renovations are a priority?"

Her front teeth worried her lower lip, giving Wade the impression she hadn't prepared at all for this *hobby.* "I'll need new fencing, corrals. A barn. A house."

"Everything's a priority?" At her nod, he said, "Give me a minute to check the balance of your trust." He entered the security codes and accessed the transaction page of her account.

Holy hell.

If his eyeballs hadn't been attached to his brain by

optic nerves they would have popped out of their sockets and bounced off his keyboard.

Sweat beaded across the bridge of Wade's nose and his glasses slipped. He shoved them back into place and gaped at the monitor, willing the numbers—any numbers—to appear.

Nothing save Samantha's name, account ID and a big fat 0 in the balance column. His fingers clicked the keyboard, searching for a transaction code that would allow him to trace the funds, but there were no notations or documentation of a bank account or wire transfer. Samantha's money had vanished into thin air.

After confiscating the roll of antacid tablets inside his desk drawer, he tossed three into his mouth and chewed furiously. Where the hell had her money gone?

He'd busted his butt for Dawson Investments and had done all his uncle had asked of him—even marrying the daughter of one of the firm's clients. His uncle had insisted the marriage would be a match made in heaven but in reality it had been a union from hell that had lasted five years too long. Since his divorce Wade had given up a social life—not that a single father had much time for one—and he'd worked twelve-hour days and most weekends. He'd get to the bottom of this mess or die trying because he wasn't giving his uncle one damned reason to pass Wade over for a promotion.

The problem had to be a computer glitch. On Monday he'd contact the firm's technology expert to resolve the issue. Until then he needed to buy time.

"What's the matter?" Samantha's question cut through Wade's panic.

"Nothing." He logged off the account. "Why?"

She pointed to the roll of antacids. "Aren't you feeling well?"

Surprised by her concern, he said, "I'm fine." Then he took a deep breath and willed his anxiety aside. "Do you have your birth certificate and a picture ID with you?" At her frown he lied. "Regulations."

"I didn't bring my birth certificate." She handed him her license.

Most people looked like goons in license photos. Samantha resembled a sultry seductress with her long black hair and a half smile that made Wade think of dark corners and slow kisses. "I believe you said you'd rather your father not be informed that you're accessing your funds." *Please don't change your mind.*

"Will that be a problem?"

"Not at all." The fewer people who knew about Samantha's visit today, the better.

"Thank you."

"Have you contacted a financial planner to assist you with managing the funds once you withdraw them?"

Her teeth nibbled her lip and her gaze shifted to the wall behind Wade. He couldn't remember Samantha being this unsure. What had happened to the young girl who'd mocked his manhood and delivered a crushing blow to his budding ego? "I'd be happy to advise you on your transactions."

"I guess that would be all right."

He blew out a deep breath. "Okay, then. I recommend withdrawing only enough money to tackle one improvement project at a time."

"I'd prefer to begin several renovations at once in order to get the ranch up and running as soon as possible."

Wade reached for the antacid tablets. He should have figured she'd make this difficult. "The well needs to be dug before anything else." Fence posts couldn't be installed without cement and water was a necessary ingredient in mixing cement.

"All right. I'll start with the well."

"In the meantime, you'll need to acquire estimates on fencing and corrals."

"Forget the estimates. I'm more concerned with getting the renovations done quickly than with saving a few hundred dollars." She rolled her eyes. "It's not like I'll run out of money."

Score one for Calamity Jane.

"How long until I receive the first check from my account?" she asked.

"Seven to ten days." Then he offered, "I've got time on my hands this weekend. I'd be happy to contact a drilling company and begin the process for you." He'd have to raid his 401(k) to pay for the well if he didn't recover her money by then.

"I appreciate your help. My brother Matt is getting married next Saturday and there's a lot going on right now."

Better her brother than Wade. He tore a piece of paper from his legal pad. "Where's the property located?"

"Southeast of the Lazy River on Route 38. It's the old Peterson farmstead. There's a mailbox at the entrance with the name painted on it." She stood, her pretty chocolate eyes skipping over him. "You'll inform me when you receive the well estimates?"

"What's your cell number?" A lengthy pause followed and Wade wondered if Samantha was worried that he'd call her asking for a date—fat chance of that happening. Women like Samantha Cartwright were out of his league. He scribbled the number she recited beneath the directions to the ranch, then handed her one of his business cards. "In case you need to get in touch with me."

Their fingers bumped, and an electrical pulse shot up Wade's arm. Samantha grasped the note, spun on her boot heels and walked out the door. Wade shook his arm to dispel the tingling sensation, certain he suffered from a pinched nerve. Samantha Cartwright was a beautiful woman but she was a client and therefore off-limits.

How had twenty million dollars vanished into thin air?

He had a week to recover Samantha's funds or he might as well kiss his promotion goodbye.

Chapter Two

When Sam exited the building, Dave the security guard drove up in her truck, radio blaring. As soon as he spotted her, he cut the music, left the engine running and hopped out. "Nice ride."

"Nice valet service."

He grinned. "Anytime."

With a wave, Sam pulled away from the curb and merged into downtown traffic. Not until she stopped at a light did she remember to turn on the GPS system. She hated driving in the city and had difficulty remembering street names and exit ramps. She tapped the screen until the favorites menu popped up. She hit Home, then concentrated on navigating traffic. After a few minutes she relaxed her grip on the wheel and merged onto I-75, passing the defunct Indian Nations Amusement Park. A few miles later she took Highway 67 to 64, breathing a sigh of relief as Tulsa faded in the rearview mirror. She flipped open her cell phone and pressed 4. Her brother's voice mail answered.

"Hey, Matt. It's me, Sam. I have a surprise. Meet me

at the Peterson homestead on Route 38. I'm forty minutes from there. But don't tell anyone, okay? Bye."

Sam wanted Matt to be the first to learn of her plans. They were as close as any brother and sister could be. He'd been there for her in the darkest hours when horrifying memories of her accident had tortured her sleep. To this day not even her father knew about the nightmares.

And if she had her way, her father would never learn about her visit to Dawson Investments. The meeting with Wade lingered in Sam's mind, frustrating her more than Wade's uncle neglecting to return her phone calls. Concentrating had been difficult in Wade's presence and she worried she'd made a fool of herself. That she couldn't remember meeting him years earlier bothered her. He must have visited the ranch around her sixteenth birthday—when she'd been kicked in the head by a horse. The weeks leading up to and following the accident had been permanently erased from her memory.

Her first impression of Wade with a *D* hadn't been very complimentary. Her job at her father's oil company often brought Sam in contact with arrogant, self-centered and opinionated businessmen. Bankers and investors considered themselves intellectually superior. Heaven forbid if they made a mistake or misjudged a situation—they'd never admit as much. But unlike most financial investors Wade had tempered his I-know-what's-best attitude with generosity—offering to contact a drilling company and obtain estimates for a well. He'd gone out of his way to help her—maybe because he'd felt guilty his uncle had ignored one of the firm's most wealthy clients. Although he'd given her no reason to trust him, she sensed Wade was an honorable man who would keep his word and not contact her father.

Genuine niceness aside, Wade was handsome in a nerdy kind of way. She'd grown up around dusty cowboys and sweaty ranchers all her life and was surprised that she'd found Wade's clean-shaven face, neatly styled hair, crisp clothes and clunky glasses attractive and…sexy. That was good and well but she had little in common with him. If she was smart she'd focus on the horse ranch and not her financial adviser.

If Sam's father caught wind of her plans he'd meddle in her affairs and guilt her into giving up her dream. She understood and sympathized with his overprotectiveness following her near brush with death and her long and arduous recovery. But the accident happened sixteen years ago. The time had come for both father and daughter to put the past behind them and move on.

For years, she'd bowed to her father's fear, allowing him to choose her path in life. No more. If her brothers, Matt and Duke, had the courage to defy their father and pursue their heart's desire, then she could do no less.

She wanted to make a difference and do something with purpose. She'd dreamed of opening a sanctuary ranch for years but worried she'd never overcome her fear of horses. She'd decided if her dream was to come true she needed to conquer her fears. A few months ago, behind her father's back, she'd begun volunteering at the Tulsa SPCA equine center. Although horses terrified Sam, her previous injury hadn't erased the memory of her love for the animals. She hoped by the time she completed renovations on the Peterson property she'd have no qualms about handling horses on her own.

Sam admitted horses alone wouldn't fill the void in her life. She dreamed of falling in love. Of finding a man willing to overlook her faults and put up with her memory lapses. With Duke happily married to Renée and living in Detroit and Matt heading down the aisle with Amy in a matter of days, Sam realized how alone she would be. Sure, her father pampered her when he was around, but his business travels took him away for weeks at a time.

Juanita, their housekeeper, generously included Sam in her family activities but it wasn't the same as having a husband of her own. One day Sam hoped to find a man who didn't want children. As much as Sam loved children—motherhood was out of the question. Never again would she allow her handicaps to cause harm to a child.

Her one serious relationship had ended in disaster when her absentmindedness had put Bo's daughter, Emily, in danger. Not even the promise of inheriting the Cartwright fortune had kept Bo from believing he and Emily were safer without Sam.

Matt had tried to heal her broken heart by setting her up on dates with his rodeo buddies. To this day, her brother wasn't aware that one of the cowboys had used Sam's forgetfulness to his advantage and had wiped out her checking account before riding off into the sunset.

Although Sam was grateful for her family's love and concern, their smothering had hindered more than helped her. The time had come to stand on her own two feet and make a play for the future she wanted—not the future others believed best for her.

The Peterson mailbox came into view and she flipped on the blinker. As the truck bumped along the rutted road she made a mental note to add a fresh layer of gravel to her ranch improvement list. Halfway to the house Matt's truck appeared in the rearview mirror.

As soon as they parked their vehicles and got out, Matt motioned to the crumbling farmhouse. "What's up with this place?"

Flinging her arms wide Sam spun in a circle. "This is my birthday present to myself."

"You've got to be kidding."

"Nope." Her smile faded at her brother's grimace. "It's not so bad," she insisted, studying the home's caved-in roof and broken windows. The outer walls leaned inward in danger of collapsing from a strong wind and the porch bowed like an old swaybacked nag. Sam's stomach churned. Had she gotten in over her head? She hated when she second-guessed herself. "Say something," she demanded at her brother's silence.

"I'm guessing Dad's in the dark about this…*present?*"

"Yes, and he'd better stay in the dark." Matt's eyes narrowed and she blurted, "I know what you're thinking."

"No, sis, you don't."

"You're wondering if this is another one of those spur-of-the-moment decisions I'm famous for making." The lingering side effects from the injury to her brain years ago weren't horrible, just a nuisance—similar to a mosquito bite. One minute you were scratching, the next you forgot about the itchy bump.

"Well, is it?" Matt demanded.

"Not at all." Once in a while she jumped the gun and made conclusions based on…well, nothing really. When she was nervous, she became forgetful, which often led to anxiety attacks. And lastly she tended to recall things out of order. She'd learned to compensate for her limitations by keeping lists and recording her activities. "I didn't make this decision lightly and I weighed the pros and cons."

"The property is a dump. When's the last time anyone lived here?" he asked.

"Twenty-five years ago."

"How long has the place been on the market?"

"Ten years."

"Give it to me straight, Sam." Matt rubbed his brow. "Why hasn't this land sold before now?"

"The well's going dry." She raised a hand to forestall any lecture. "I'm aware that I'll need a source of water if I intend to board horses."

"Horses?" Her brother's face paled.

Samantha squeezed his arm. "Promise you won't tell Daddy, but I've been working with horses at the SPCA and I'm feeling more confident around them." She sucked in a deep breath, grateful her brother hadn't interrupted. "I intend to board horses that the SPCA can't find foster homes for."

Matt studied her, then he brushed a strand of hair from her face and asked, "Will you have help?" He really wanted to know if there would be someone to watch over her.

"I plan to hire a couple of hands."

Her answer appeared to satisfy him because he

changed the subject. "Tell me you had a drilling company confirm a second water source before you signed the closing papers."

"Better than that," she boasted. "I checked with Millicent, the resident water witch." Sam had witnessed the old woman's dousing stick wiggle and shake when they'd walked the property.

"What do you mean *resident?*"

Sam pointed beyond the barn to a shanty near a huge hackberry tree.

"That hovel's hardly habitable."

"Millicent's lived on the property all her life. Her parents were sharecroppers."

"Why hasn't she packed her things and left?"

"She has nowhere to go." Sam shrugged. "She's not hurting anything by staying." Having remained under her father's roof all these years, Sam was leery of living alone and looked forward to having a neighbor when she set up house on the property.

Matt frowned and she sensed he struggled with wanting to support her and at the same time protect her. And she loved him dearly for caring. "What about your nightmares?" he asked.

Once in a while Sam's nightmares were so vivid she woke screaming—a silent scream her father never heard. But Matt had sensed his sister's night terrors and had held her until she'd fallen back to sleep. As the years passed, the nightmares occurred less frequently, holding off for months at a time until Matt arrived home from the rodeo circuit.

"I haven't had a nightmare in over a year," she lied. Last night she'd awoken soaked in sweat and gasping for breath. "I want—" tears welled in her eyes and she brushed them away "—need this ranch."

Matt hugged her. "Dad's going to blow a gasket."

"Daddy isn't going to find out." She hoped. "At least not right away."

"Maybe I can talk Amy into staying at the Lazy River after we're married. We could help—"

"No. I'm doing this on my own."

"Where is the money coming from?"

"My trust fund." She crinkled her nose. "Now that I'm thirty-two, I can withdraw money without Daddy's permission. After the wedding he leaves for Europe. By the time he returns, I'll have made significant progress and then I'll break the news to him."

"You're really going to do this, aren't you?" Matt held her gaze.

"You and Duke got your dreams—I want mine."

"We'll worry about you living here all alone."

"I'm not alone."

"That's right, your closest neighbor is a witch." Matt yanked her ponytail. "C'mon. We'd better head home. Duke and Renée are flying in for your birthday."

One brother down. One to go.

WHEN SAM PULLED INTO the Lazy River ranch yard, she noticed her father's 1959 two-door black-and-chrome Chevrolet Apache pickup parked near the house. Although Dominick Cartwright could afford any car in the world, he had a soft spot for old Chevy trucks. And right now Samantha's nephew sat behind the wheel, pretending to drive.

Duke and Renée had adopted Timmy shortly after

they'd married this past February. The little boy had been in the Detroit foster care system his entire life. Sam was thrilled he'd gotten his wish for a family and she loved playing the role of favorite aunt. After Matt married Amy, Samantha would add two nieces to her brood—Rose and Lily. As much as she loved hanging around the children, they were a painful reminder that this was as close to motherhood as she'd come.

Sam parked her truck, then headed for the old Apache.

"Happy birthday, brat," Duke called.

"Daddy said you weren't arriving until the wedding next week." She bear-hugged her stepbrother, then poked her head through the truck window and planted a big, loud smooch on Timmy's cheek.

"Gross, Aunt Sammy!" Timmy made a big production of wiping germs off his cheek.

"I didn't want to miss your birthday," Duke said.

Before her stepbrother had met Renée he couldn't get far enough away from the Cartwright ranch. Sam credited Renée with softening Duke's attitude toward children and family.

"I'm glad you're here." Then she added, "Maybe Renée will convince Amy to allow Daddy to invite more guests to the wedding. Amy wants to keep the reception small enough to have at the house and Daddy wants to move things to the Crowne Plaza Hotel in Tulsa."

Duke chuckled. "Sounds like the old man."

"Got a minute to talk?"

"Sure." Duke opened the truck door. "Timmy, go see if Aunt Amy needs help with Rose or Lily."

"Girls are so lame."

"Oh, c'mon. Lily's a cutie," Sam said.

"Uncle Matt told me Lily poops marbles in her pants. That's gross." Timmy marched off, grumbling under his breath.

"Let's take a walk." Sam slipped her arm through Duke's and they strolled toward the barn. "How's life in Detroit?"

"Renée's working with a local teacher to create a homeschooling program for the kids who end up in Santa's Shelter when the doors open this September."

"What's happened to the kids you discovered hiding in your warehouse this past Christmas?" Aside from Timmy, Sam couldn't remember their names.

"Renée's keeping a close eye on the group. Mrs. Jensen suffered a mild heart attack a few months ago and Renée worried that she'd have to find a new home for Crystal and Evie. Crystal surprised everyone by stepping up and caring for the other children while Mrs. Jensen recovered." Duke chuckled. "Crystal even ditched the gothic clothes and dyed her hair back to blond."

"Wasn't there a teenage boy in the group?"

"José. He never surfaced after running away from the Covenant House, but a few weeks ago Renée found a note in our mailbox with the words *I'm okay* scribbled on it."

"From José?"

"We can't be sure but the paper smelled like cigarette smoke and Renée was never able to convince José to quit the cigarettes."

They stopped at the bench outside the barn and sat. "Willie's story took an interesting turn," Duke continued.

Sam wracked her brain but couldn't recall a boy named Willie.

"Willie's birth dad entered the picture and not by

choice. Evidently the young man wasn't aware that he'd gotten Willie's mom pregnant."

"Is he going to raise Willie?"

"Not sure. It's a tabloid mess. Willie's father is white and the son of Richard McDaniel, a prominent plastic surgeon in Detroit."

"How did the story become public?"

"You'll have to ask Renée for the details but apparently a disgruntled patient of McDaniel's leaked the information to the press."

"Where's Willie now?"

Duke chuckled. "Living at the McDaniel mansion. Willie's father is in college and his grandfather's divorced, so the boy's under the supervision of the McDaniel housekeeper."

"Wasn't there one more child?" Sam asked.

"Ricci. He was arrested for street racing. His foster family gave up on him and Renée had to place him in a boy's orphanage. His probation officer keeps a close eye on him, but Renée believes it's only a matter of time before he runs away and joins a gang."

Sam couldn't imagine the day-to-day emotional upheaval her sister-in-law experienced as a social worker. "Renée's a special woman."

"I'm lucky to have Renée even though I share her with hundreds of kids," he said.

"What about your condo? When do you two plan to move in?" Her brother had purchased an old warehouse along Detroit's riverfront. Company offices and a condo were to occupy the top two floors while the rest housed a recreational center and shelter for homeless children.

"Renée and I decided against the condo."

"Really?"

"We want our kids to grow up in a neighborhood with other families. And Renée worried about moving away from her mother. For now we're keeping Renée's house and making plans to expand."

"You said kids as in plural."

Duke grinned. "Don't tell anyone but Renée's pregnant."

"Oh, Duke, that's wonderful!" Sam fought a pang of envy as she hugged her brother. "When is she due?"

"Middle of January."

"Is Timmy excited?"

"He doesn't know yet and we don't want to make the news public until after Timmy's surgery at the end of August."

The boy had been born with a clubfoot but because he'd been shuffled from one foster home to another through the years he'd never had the deformity corrected.

"Would you call me when Timmy checks into the hospital? I'd like to send him a gift to cheer him up."

"Sure thing." Duke cleared his throat. "Matt hasn't known Amy or her daughters long. Has he said much about their relationship?"

Sam laughed. "You're one to talk. You met Renée in December and married her in February." Her teasing remark earned her a pinch on the arm. "Hey!"

"How does Matt feel about inheriting an instant family?"

"How did you feel about marrying a woman who'll always be involved with other people's children?" Sam countered.

"Touché." Duke chuckled. "That Rose sure is opinionated and Lily, with her blond curls, is nothing but a handful of cute."

Sam's turn to share her personal news. "I bought the old Peterson homestead on Route 38 two weeks ago."

"I'm listening," Duke said, offering his undivided attention.

That's what she loved about her stepbrother—he never rushed to judgment like Matt did. Duke heard a person out before offering an opinion. "I need to be part of a worthwhile cause. I hate working in Daddy's office. There are days I can't breathe let alone concentrate."

"I'm sorry, Sam."

"For what?"

"I should have taken your complaints more seriously when you came to Detroit before Christmas. I could have spoken with Dominick."

"I wasn't ready to do anything then. But I am now," she insisted, hoping to reassure herself as well as her brother.

"What exactly are you doing?" he asked.

"The same thing you and Renée have done for homeless kids, except I'm opening a sanctuary for neglected and abandoned horses."

"An admirable cause but are you ready to work with horses again?"

"Yes." She didn't have a choice—not if she intended to move on with her life. She needed to put her fears to rest if she wanted to experience again the special relationship with a horse that she'd always treasured. "I've been visiting the SPCA equine center for several months."

"Does Dominick know you're hanging around horses?"

"No," she admitted, then rushed on. "Daddy would have made a big fuss if I'd told him. I'm taking things slow and working with horses that are mild-tempered." For now. She eventually wanted to help all horses—even the unpredictable ones.

"Does Matt approve?"

"He's having fits because the property's in poor condition and with the wedding preparations he doesn't have time to help out."

"I could—"

"Thanks but I don't need help from a man who can't pound a nail without hitting his thumb."

Duke mussed her hair, then smiled. "You've got a big heart."

"So do you, Duke. Or else you wouldn't be sharing your warehouse with homeless kids."

"If you need help making financial decisions—"

"Thanks, but Wade Dawson volunteered to handle my money."

"Dawson is your financial adviser?"

She nodded. "His uncle owns Dawson Investments."

"Do you trust him?"

She had no choice—not if she wanted to prevent her father from discovering her plans. "He's competent." *Good-looking.* "And he's insisting I withdraw money on an as-needed basis to keep the balance of my savings earning interest."

"Smart man."

Trusting men outside her family wasn't easy for Sam. But Wade made her want to believe he wouldn't take advantage of her—even if he discovered her short-comings.

Sam would never allow another man—even a nerdy one—to make her feel that vulnerable ever again.

Chapter Three

"That's insane!" Wade shouted into the phone. The drilling company he'd contacted after Samantha Cartwright had left his office yesterday phoned back with a quote for the Peterson homestead—a hundred dollars per square foot drilled and an estimated drill depth to hit water of 1,100 feet. A $110,000 may not be a big deal to a Cartwright but it was a damned big deal to Wade, whose retirement fund would take a hit until he recovered Samantha's money.

"What do you mean you'll have to use diamond bits?" The company manager droned on about the pricey bits needed to break through bedrock. Then he spewed data from well logs of properties in the area to justify his cost.

The one thing preventing Wade from suffering cardiac arrest was the news that the first available drill date for the property was early September. Wade suspected if he mentioned the Cartwright name the owner would rearrange the company's schedule and break ground tomorrow. Wade remained silent. He needed more time to investigate Samantha's trust fund debacle.

Numerous calls to his uncle had gone unreturned, which was out of character for the old man. Whatever his uncle was up to, Wade didn't appreciate being left in the dark.

When the manager offered to reserve a date in September, Wade declined. "I'll be in touch." He snapped his cell phone shut and stared out his condo window at downtown Tulsa. His conscience nagged—to inform Samantha about the missing funds or not? Wade's job, his future at Dawson Investments, his position in the family—too much was at stake.

In the end it was Wade's personal financial situation that made the decision for him—he didn't have $110,000 to pay the drilling company. Three years ago his ex-wife, Carmen, had walked away from their marriage with half his 401(k). She'd also gotten their home and a hefty child-support check each month. After purchasing his condo and furnishing the rooms, Wade had all but drained his retirement portfolio.

Then his son had begun having problems when he'd entered first grade. Wade remembered what it had been like to be the kid who didn't fit in. Luke's genius IQ made relating to his peers difficult. Carmen had insisted Luke would adjust, but Wade had refused to stand aside while the boy suffered teasing and ridicule. Wade enrolled his son in the Tulsa Boys Academy—a private school for overachievers and high-intellect children.

The cost of tuition was another reason he hadn't been able to sock money away. Wade didn't care because Luke thrived at the academy and enjoyed learning in a challenging and stimulating environment.

Wade was determined to keep his son in the school even if he became penniless in the process.

Luke strolled into the living room, carrying his favorite book—*The Chronicles of Narnia: Prince Caspian.* Although it was only 8:00 a.m. on a Saturday, Luke had been up reading for an hour. "What's the matter, Dad?"

"Nothing." Wade's chest tightened with love at his son's concern. The boy was a miniature replica of himself right down to his choice of reading material. Wade had spent his childhood with his head buried in books—fantasy had been better than real life. Even though Luke had enrolled in a summer school literature program at the academy, Wade hated to see his son spend the entire weekend reading.

Wade had custody of Luke every weekend and the two used the time together to do guy stuff—like bowling or attending a professional soccer game. They'd gone fishing once, but Wade hadn't been able to untangle the lines, so they'd tossed their poles in the trash and spent the afternoon at the condominium's swimming pool. "You up for a car ride in the country?"

Luke adjusted his glasses and shrugged. "I guess."

Wade eyed the boy's khaki shorts and short-sleeved Polo shirt. Carmen dressed Luke like a Dapper Dan doll. Maybe if his son tore the pockets on his pants or smudged his shirt Carmen would think twice about purchasing expensive outfits for an eight-year-old. Then Wade glanced at himself and cringed. He wasn't much of a role model in his khaki pants, loafers and short-sleeved cotton Oxford shirt.

"Where are we going?" Luke asked.

Scooping the car keys from the ceramic bowl on the coffee table, Wade said, "To an old farm." Assuming Samantha would be occupied with her brother's wedding plans, he intended to check out the Peterson place. With any luck he'd devise a plan to convince Samantha to hold off on her pet project—at least until he spoke with his uncle.

"Can I bring my book?"

"Sure." His son lugged books around like other kids carried iPods and cell phones in their pockets. Wade knew for a fact that Luke had read *The Chronicles of Narnia* series three times already.

Fifteen minutes later Wade left the Tulsa city limits behind. He lowered the car windows, the hot afternoon breeze ruffling Luke's hair and flipping the pages of his book. "Look out there." Wade pointed to the grazing cattle. "That's a huge herd."

Luke watched the animals for all of three seconds before burying his head in the book again.

So much for distracting his son. Wade closed the windows and adjusted the air conditioner. Left alone with his own musings, Samantha's face popped into his mind—an annoying habit of late. Her dark eyes and high cheekbones were bold, exotic…*striking*.

A warm throb pulsed between his thighs. When was the last time a woman had stirred him physically, and why did that woman have to be Samantha Cartwright? The cowgirl hadn't even remembered him.

The women he'd gravitated toward in the past shared few traits with the oil baron's daughter. Yesterday he'd been caught off guard by the vulnerability in

Samantha's gaze—the look hadn't been there when they'd met years ago. What had happened to the girl whose stare had intimidated Wade and whose words had challenged him to climb a tree he had no business scaling? Not even after he'd fallen and broken his arm had she uttered an apology. Whatever the cause for the change in Samantha's demeanor he hoped her congeniality lasted until he located her money.

He spotted the Peterson mailbox along Route 38 and turned onto a dirt road laden with potholes. Samantha had her priorities out of order. If she wanted a new well dug, first the road needed to be regraded and topped with several inches of fresh gravel so the drilling trucks could drive onto the property. The BMW's suspension survived the bumpy ride and Wade parked in front of the crumbling farmhouse.

Book forgotten, Luke pressed his nose to the windshield and gaped. "Is it haunted?"

"Maybe. No one's lived here for years." His mind quickly calculated the cost of building a new house if Samantha stuck to her goal to turn this place into a horse sanctuary. The barn wasn't much better—half the roof was missing and immense holes peppered the sides. A crumbling brick silo stood off in the distance. The property was in worse shape than Samantha had let on. No wonder she wanted to keep her father in the dark about her plans.

"Dad, there's an old lady sitting under that tree."

The resident water witch. "C'mon," Wade said. "We'll introduce ourselves." The granny didn't budge from her rocker as they approached. "Hello," Wade called. "You must be Millicent."

Cloudy gray eyes peered at Wade through a wrinkled face that resembled a Chinese shar-pei. "Who wants to know?"

"I'm Wade Dawson, Samantha Cartwright's financial adviser." He held out his hand and the old woman hesitated before offering hers. The digits crooked at odd angles and her knuckles were swollen and red with inflammation. Taking care, Wade squeezed gently.

"If ya folks is lookin' fer Sam, she ain't here."

Before Wade explained his visit, Luke blurted, "How old are you?"

"Well now, I ain't sure." Millicent spat tobacco juice at the ground, barely missing Wade's shoes. "I reckon somewhere's 'round a hundred."

"Wow, that's cool." Luke squinted through his glasses. "The cost of a first-class stamp when you were born was just two cents."

Although Wade enjoyed listening to his son spew trivia off the top of his head, most people didn't. More often than not intelligence earned enemies not friends.

Millicent narrowed her eyes until the wrinkles on her face swallowed them whole. "What else ya knows 'bout 1909?"

"Skee-Ball was invented by J. D. Estes in Philadelphia. And the U.S. issued the first Lincoln penny."

When Luke paused, the old woman said, "Go on, youngin'. I'm listenin'."

"The 1909 Model T Ford was one of the fifty worst cars of all time."

"I wouldn't know 'bout that. My daddy didn't have no car."

"Did you ever own a car?" Luke asked.

"Son, that's none of—"

"Shush now." Millicent waved a knobby hand in the air, excluding Wade from the conversation. "Years ago Mr. Peterson gave me his 1953 Bel-Air."

"What happened to the car?"

"It's over yonder in the barn."

Wade shielded his eyes against the glaring sun and stared at the dilapidated structure. "You're storing a Bel-Air in that barn?" It was a miracle a strong wind hadn't blown the structure down.

"Said so, didn't I?" The granny grunted.

Before Wade had a chance to ask about the antique car the sound of a diesel truck engine met his ears. A large four-by-four extended cab pickup stopped next to his BMW. Samantha sat behind the wheel.

Damn. The last person he wanted to run into today was the rich cowgirl.

SAM GRIPPED THE STEERING WHEEL until her knuckles ached. All those stupid female fantasies she'd nurtured since meeting Wade yesterday had been run over and flattened when she spotted the little boy at his side. Of all the scenarios she'd envisioned of her and Wade there had never been a child in any of them.

Go figure. The one man who'd piqued her interest, since her disastrous relationship with Bo, had a child. Kids weren't part of Samantha's future, so that meant Wade wasn't, either. Swallowing her disappointment, she hopped out of the truck and headed toward the group gathered beneath the hackberry tree.

"Hello, Wade." Sam glanced at the boy and then looked away. The memory of Bo's daughter wandering off while in her care forced Sam to retreat a step, increasing the space between her and the child.

"Samantha, I'd like you to meet my son, Luke. Luke, this is Ms. Cartwright. She owns the property."

There was no mistaking the resemblance between father and son. The miniature male possessed Wade's dark hair, dark eyes, square chin and even the same black-rimmed geeky glasses—not to mention they wore similar outfits.

The boy flashed a crooked smile and waved his hand. "Hi."

"Pleasure to meet you, Luke." She switched her attention to Millicent. "You doing okay?"

"Jest shootin' the bull." The old woman pushed herself out of the rocker. "Best be headin' inside." Millicent shuffled toward the clapboard shanty.

"Wait!" Sam and Wade spoke at the same time.

Embarrassed by her outburst, Sam sputtered, "No need to leave on our account." Wade unnerved her and she needed Millicent to act as a buffer between her and the financial guru. "What brings you out to the Last Chance Ranch?" she asked Wade.

"The what?"

"I'm calling my horse sanctuary Last Chance Ranch." The ranch wasn't only a last resort for unwanted horses but also an opportunity for Sam to finally strike out on her own.

"I stopped by to get an idea of the amount of work that needs to be done on the place." His mouth twisted into a grimace. "There must be a hundred small spreads in the area in better condition than this."

Sam admitted the property was in poor shape, but

that's why she'd bought the place below market value. She flashed a smug smile. "Now you understand why I need my trust fund money sooner rather than later."

"Speaking of money," Wade said, "I contacted a drilling company after you left the office yesterday. They phoned with a bid this morning."

"How much?" she asked.

"A hundred dollars per foot drilled and the well comps in this area put the water table between a thousand and twelve-hundred feet."

"That's $110,000," the boy blurted.

Good grief. The details had barely registered in Sam's head before the little genius had spouted a dollar amount.

"The cost doesn't include testing the water or capping the well." Wade nodded toward the ranch road. "The potholes need to be filled and new gravel laid down before heavy trucks drive in here."

"When can the drilling company break ground?" What was a hundred grand when she had millions?

"They're booked solid until September."

Panic pumped through Sam's bloodstream and she forced herself to breathe in deeply through her nose. In…out. In…out. Becoming upset would lead to confusion and forgetfulness and she refused to make a fool of herself in front of Wade. Even though they had no future, she didn't want him to believe she was a ditz. "The well can't wait until September." The faster she got the ranch up and running, the less chance her father would interfere with her plans. Sam had a nasty habit of backing down when confronted by her father. "I'll phone the company Monday morning and offer more money."

Wade's face lost color. "Don't waste your money on bribes," he insisted. "Acquiring the necessary permits to drill will take time."

"Bunch o' nonsense if ya ask me," Millicent said, inviting herself into the conversation. "Don't need no machine to show ya where the water is." She rolled her lips over her gum. "The water ain't no thousand feet down, neither."

Sam cleared her throat. "Millicent is a dowser."

"You mentioned that yesterday," Wade said.

Oh. She'd forgotten.

"What's a dowser?" Luke pushed his glasses up his nose and squinted through the lenses.

"I'll show ya. First, I gots to find a divinin' rod." Millicent wandered off toward the barn.

"A what?" Luke asked his father.

"A magic stick—" Sam answered for Wade "—that shakes and wiggles when it senses water below the ground."

"Folklore, son." Wade shook his head.

"Maybe, but Millicent doesn't charge a hundred thousand dollars for her services."

"What's the going rate for a water witch?" he asked.

"A can of coffee and a pouch of tobacco would probably suffice."

"After you." Wade swept his arm out in front of him.

Sam followed Millicent, the big geek and the little geek trailing behind.

WADE WISHED HE'D NEVER suggested a drive in the country this morning. He'd rather be in his comfortable, air-conditioned condo reading Friday's *Wall Street*

Journal instead of tromping through prickly weeds in ninety-degree heat while an old granny poked the ground with a tree branch. He doubted any psychic could detect a drop of moisture in this mini dust bowl. Another gust of wind blew dirt in his face, forcing him to remove his glasses and wipe them against his shirt.

The water witch stopped beneath a tree and stared up the trunk. "What's wrong?" he asked, impatient to end the hoax.

Luke peered at Wade through dusty glasses. "Millicent's looking for a stick."

Wade removed his son's glasses, cleaned them off, then handed them back. "Won't any stick do?" he asked Samantha. The old biddy had a habit of ignoring him.

Samantha leaned near and whispered, "A willow or peach tree switch works best for dowsing." The scent of honeysuckle drifted up Wade's nose, distracting him. He decided the sweet smell came from Samantha's shampoo.

"Is that a peach tree?" Wade curled his fingers into a fist to keep from touching Samantha's dark hair, which glistened beneath the hot sun.

Before Samantha had answered his question, Millicent spoke. "This here's the one." The granny pointed to a branch five feet above the gray bun on her head, then settled her rheumy eyes on Wade. "Don't stand there, ya dope, climb up 'n fetch me that twig."

Was she nuts? Wade glanced at Samantha. The last time he'd climbed a tree he'd fallen on his ass in front of a teenage girl. This time he was a grown man. The teenager was a beautiful woman. And he'd probably land on his ass again.

"I'll get it," Samantha volunteered.

Aw, hell. He studied his leather loafers—his tread-less weekend shoes—and silently cursed. "Wait." He stepped in front of Samantha and searched the tree trunk for a foothold.

"If I give you a shove, you'll be able to grab that lower limb." Samantha inched closer.

Although he liked the idea of Samantha's hands on his rump, with his luck her hold would slip and catch him in the nuts and he'd land at her feet curled up in a ball of misery. "I'm too heavy."

"What about me, Dad? I can reach the branch."

To Wade's knowledge, his son had never climbed a tree in his life. "I don't—"

"Hoist the boy onto yer shoulders." Millicent glared at Wade, daring him to defy her.

"Luke's never—"

"Give him a chance, Wade." Samantha grasped his arm, her gaze imploring. He appreciated that she stuck up for his son, but it was the pleading expression on Luke's face that tore at Wade. Climbing a tree was an adventure, the kind Luke read about in books but had never experienced. "Be careful."

Luke's grin went straight to Wade's heart. "I won't get hurt, I promise."

Throat tight, Wade stood aside while Samantha gave his son a crash course on the dos and don'ts of tree climbing. Then she bent at the waist and cupped her hands. Luke placed his foot in the hold and Samantha hoisted him high enough to seize a lower branch.

"Now step on my shoulder, Luke," she instructed.

"Here." Wade offered his shoulder. When Luke pulled himself onto a thick branch that held his weight,

Wade released his legs. As he lowered his arms, Wade's hand brushed Samantha's breast and she sucked in a quiet breath. "I'm—"

"Dad, I did it!" Luke's shout saved Wade from an embarrassing apology.

"Hold tight!" Out of the corner of Wade's eye he noticed Samantha's rosy cheeks. Darn it. The blunder had happened quickly, leaving only a sensation of softness lingering on his fingertips.

"Git that branch to yer right." A craggy voice ordered.

Luke touched the limb Millicent indicated. "That's the one, boy. Snap it off cleanlike."

"I can't," Luke complained after several attempts to break the branch.

"Twirl it one way, then the other fer a bit."

"What about a different branch?" Wade raised his arms ready to catch Luke should his son lose his balance.

"Nope. Gotta have that one."

Face scrunched in determination, Luke fought the branch until his glasses slipped off his nose and fell to the ground.

Samantha scooped them up.

Time to end the adventure. Luke was blind without his glasses. "That's enough, son. Lean over and I'll catch you."

"No, Dad. I can do this. I promise."

"Quit pesterin' the boy." Millicent glared.

"Give him a little bit longer, Wade. He's almost got it," Samantha said.

Wade wasn't used to being ganged up on. Luke was

so far out of his element not even his brilliant mind would save him if he made one wrong move. A moment later...

"I did it!" Luke shouted, swaying sideways on the limb as he waved the switch above his head.

"Sit still, afore ya fall on yer face."

Luke handed the branch to Millicent, who inspected her dowsing tool with great care, then pronounced, "This'll do," and walked off.

"Roll onto your stomach and lower your legs while hanging on to the limb," Samantha said.

His son followed her instructions, then Wade grabbed him around the waist. "Let go." He lowered Luke to the ground. Samantha handed over the eyeglasses and as soon as Luke put them on he tore after Millicent.

"Guess my son's a better tree climber than his father." Wade smiled sheepishly. He expected at least a murmur of agreement from Samantha, not a blank stare.

"You don't remember, do you?" he asked.

"Remember what?"

"You challenged me to a tree-climbing contest at the Lazy River Ranch when you were in high school and I was in college. I fell out of the tree and broke my arm. You called me a wimp."

Her beautiful eyes widened, then without a word she spun and walked off.

She really doesn't remember me.

Chapter Four

Darn it. Wade refused to drop the tree-climbing incident.

Okay. Years ago he'd fallen out of a tree and had broken his arm while visiting the Cartwright ranch. *Big deal.*

Sam stomped toward the barn, the nerdy financial investor dogging her boot heels. Her memory lapse had bruised Wade's ego, confirming her suspicion that the man hadn't heard about her near-death experience with a horse. If she had her way, he'd remain in the dark about that period in her life. She feared if he learned she suffered lingering effects from the head trauma, he'd alert her father and attempt to put a stop to her plans for the Peterson homestead. And she for darn sure didn't care for Wade's pity—she'd been on the receiving end of enough sympathetic stares to last a lifetime.

Mr. Financial Adviser exasperated and intrigued Sam. Wade was a nice change from her brother's rodeo friends and the roughnecks who worked on her father's oil rigs. An aura of sophistication surrounded Wade. His neatly styled hair, clean, crisp dress shirts and sexy cologne stirred her as no other man ever had.

Good grief, Sam. Wade has a son, which means he's married and off-limits. Besides, converting this property into a horse ranch was her first priority. There would be time later for setting her sights on a man to share her life and dreams with.

She skirted the corner of the barn, Wade following as he swatted at a black fly buzzing his head. She swallowed a chuckle. *Next time don't wear cologne.* Better yet he should stay in his corporate office and let her deal with the property renovations.

"Ya see the best chance o' findin' water is with a fresh-cut switch. Ya got to have a fork in the branch like a Y shape or it's bad luck."

"How does the stick find the water?" Luke asked.

"It jest knows."

"A stick can't just know," Luke argued. "There's gotta be a scientific reason for the twig's power."

"Don't know nothin' 'bout science. Jest magic."

The boy gaped. "You have magical powers?"

"Some folks calls me a water witch."

Luke shrugged. "You do kinda look like a witch. You're old and you have lots of wrinkles."

Sam smothered a smile behind her hand. Little Einstein was honest if nothing else.

"Years o' pickin' sugar beets and beans in the sun give me a face full o' lines."

"But you're not mean like the witches I read about in books."

"Enough talk about witches, Luke." Wade's comment earned him a glower from Millicent.

"Tell me how the stick finds water." Luke slid his glasses up his nose.

"The stick don't. I finds the water." Millicent closed her eyes and said, "First, I quiet my mind."

"Don't your eyes have to be open to see?"

"Shush now, boy. I sees everythin' in my head." No one moved, then Millicent whispered, "I'm searchin' fer an ol' time well made o' stone with a windlass fer haulin' water a bucketful at a time."

Shielding his eyes from the sun's glare, Luke scanned the horizon, looking for a well that was visible only in Millicent's mind.

"Once I sees the well I gots to approach with care." The old woman stood frozen, eyes closed, arms stretched before her. After a moment she walked off, veering left of the barn. Luke hurried to catch up. Wade followed his son and Sam traipsed after Wade, content to breathe in his sexy scent.

Millicent stopped and extended the dowsing stick. Waited. Then reversed direction. Eyes closed, she moved farther away from the barn. Twenty yards later she stopped again—the forked end of the stick quivered, then dropped toward the ground at her feet.

"Did she find water?" Wade inched closer and Sam noticed gold flecks in his brown eyes. The man had a habit of invading her personal space—an odd thing for a married man to do.

"I believe so." Sam glanced at Wade's left hand and noticed his bare ring finger. Which meant nothing. Lots of married men refused to wear rings.

Bending over, Millicent tugged fistfuls of grass from the earth. Luke dropped to his knees and helped. Once the bare dirt had been exposed, Millicent patted the ground. "Here." She pressed Luke's palm to the spot.

"Feel that?" Then she moved the boy's hand to another area. "Feel that?"

"This one's cooler." Luke returned his hand to the first spot.

"Water under the ground makes the dirt cold," Millicent explained.

Sam ignored Wade's eye roll and asked, "How far down do you think the water is?"

"Sixty feet."

Millicent's claim lured a snort from Wade. Typical geek—always demanding evidence to back up facts.

"Dad. You gotta feel this," Luke said. "Millicent's right. The ground's colder here—" he patted the earth "—than over there."

Wade surprised Sam when he did as his son requested. Brow furrowed, Wade squatted and pressed his palm to the ground, drawing Sam's attention to his hand. Her mind wandered along a path of its own as her eyes followed the movement of his lean fingers, imagining them stroking her skin, palming her breast, touching her...*there*.

Wade stood, then slapped at the dust on his hands, the sound ending Sam's fantasy. "Are you sure there's water?" he asked Millicent.

"Ya callin' me a liar?" The old woman waved the switch in the air and Sam feared she intended to smack Wade with the branch.

"A sixty-foot hole can't be that difficult to dig." Wade studied the ground.

"Oh, no," Sam said. "You're not—"

Wade's gaze shifted from the ground to Sam's face. "Why pay a drilling company over a hundred thousand dollars when we can dig the well ourselves?"

"We?" Sam had no intention of shoveling dirt. There were too many other items on her to-do list that needed to be tackled.

"Yes, you and me," Wade confirmed.

Luke jumped up and down. "I can help, too!"

"What do you say?" Wade's eyes lit with excitement. If playing in the dirt thrilled the man this much, then he needed a vacation from his job.

Hating to see the boy get his hopes up, Sam said, "I doubt your mom would want you to risk getting hurt, Luke."

"My mom won't care. Besides I spend most of my time with my dad."

Confused, Sam glanced at Wade and he said, "Luke's mom and I are divorced."

That explained the absence of a ring, but not the twitter of excitement that raced through Sam. Her gaze traveled over Wade's body. "You're not exactly the well-digging type." The sparkle dimmed in his eyes and Sam cursed herself for being blunt, then shrugged off her concern—no way would a man like Wade care what she thought of him. "I'm not worried about saving money," she insisted. "Now that Millicent located the water, the drilling company should be able to dig and cap the well in less than a day."

"Permits take time," he argued.

"Not that long. I'll phone the owner of the company and ask if they can squeeze—"

"You said you didn't want your father learning about this ranch until you'd whipped it into shape. How will you keep the news from him if you hire professionals?"

Why hadn't Sam considered this complication

before? As soon as the drilling company learned the client was a Cartwright they'd contact her father. No one dug a hole anywhere in Oklahoma without Dominick Cartwright being informed.

"C'mon, Samantha. People dug wells by hand all the time in the olden—" Wade glanced at Millicent.

"Watch yerself," the witch warned.

"I'll research how to dig a well," Luke chimed in.

Sam nibbled her lip, unsure how to proceed.

"Please," Luke begged.

Wade's son was so darned cute she hadn't the heart to upset him. Once her father flew off to Europe, she'd be free to contact a drilling company if the do-it-yourself well-digging project came to a standstill. "Fine. Let's begin digging next Sunday."

"Why not Saturday?" Wade asked.

"My brother's wedding is Saturday." Hadn't she mentioned Matt's wedding to Wade? "We'll meet here bright and early Sunday morning."

"It's a date," Wade confirmed.

A date? She supposed digging a well was about as exciting a date as any for a nerd.

"UNCLE CHARLES, I ASSURE YOU this is no snafu," Wade argued over the telephone Monday evening. After three days of leaving voice mails and text messages, the man had finally surfaced.

"Now, Wade—"

He hated when his uncle used that tone with him— as if Wade was a ten-year-old boy.

"Have my secretary—"

Veronica the airhead.

"—check with our systems analyst. The man's sharp as a whip."

Implying Wade was not. "I've already put a call in to the man."

"Good. He'll fix the commuter glitch and you'll be fine." His uncle congratulated his golf partner on a nice putt, then resumed the conversation. "My boy, if you're hoping for a vice president position you'll have to prove you're capable of handling a crisis on your own."

"Aren't you the least interested in learning which client's money is missing?" His uncle hadn't asked, making Wade suspicious. He couldn't believe his uncle would intentionally tamper with a client's portfolio unless the old man intended to put Wade through some kind of test before offering a promotion.

"I trust you to handle the situation."

Even though his uncle professed to be proud of Wade's accomplishments, Wade suspected the man was irritated that his nephew had ended up working for Dawson Investments and not his son, Jarrod, who'd shocked the family with his marriage to Richard. The happy couple lived in California and rarely kept in touch with the family.

"When do you intend to return to the office?" Wade asked.

"Not for a while. I'm heading to Dubai after I leave Scotland."

The firm had no clients in Dubai. Maybe his uncle hoped to land an account there. They'd need a new client or two or three, not to mention a good lawyer if Dawson Investments was held responsible for Samantha Cartwright's missing millions. "I'll keep you posted on what the systems analyst says."

"Don't do anything rash, young man." *Click.*

Wade scrutinized his reflection in the floor-to-ceiling glass windows of his condo and wondered if his uncle would ever view him as anything other than the needy kid he'd been forced to take in upon his sister's death. Wade doubted he'd ever earn enough points with his uncle to gain forgiveness for whatever sins his mother had committed against the family. Maybe it was time he stop trying.

"Look, Dad." Luke waltzed into the living room and spread an assortment of papers on the coffee table. "Instructions on how to dig a well." After visiting Samantha's property, his son had spent hours researching information on water witches, dowsing and digging wells the old-fashioned way—by hand.

"I see you've been surfing the Net again," Wade said.

"Yep."

Before his son spouted off a million facts and figures, he asked, "Did you check in with your mother?"

For the past year Carmen had neglected the visitation schedule they'd agreed upon in the divorce settlement. Instead of Wade spending weekends with his son, Luke often remained the entire week when Carmen traveled with her new fiancé. Not that Wade complained. He enjoyed spending extra time with his son. He never broached the subject with Luke, but Wade suspected when Carmen married again she'd ask Wade to assume full custody of their son.

"I texted Mom. She said hi."

Wade doubted Carmen had bothered to send along a greeting, but appreciated that Luke cared about his father's feelings. "Okay, let's see your research." Wade sat on the sofa and perused the documents. He'd convinced Samantha that digging a well by hand would be faster and cheaper than hiring professionals. He hoped to hell he'd been right. "Give me the short version, Luke."

"We dig a round hole four feet across. And you're supposed to keep checking the sides of the well while you dig to make sure the walls don't cave in."

Good point. If he ended up buried beneath a hundred pounds of Oklahoma red clay he'd never locate Samantha's missing money. "Then what?"

"Once the hole is too deep to toss the shovelful of dirt over the side you have to rig up a bucket system."

"Does it show a picture?" Wade studied the sketch of the crude pulley system Luke handed him.

"When you hit water," his son continued, "you have to use a different kind of shovel."

"Oh?"

"A flat one with a short handle."

"Anything else?"

"We need a spud bar to pry rocks loose and a clam-shell posthole digger."

Luke droned on about installing casings to prevent the sides of the hole from caving in, but Wade's mind wandered to Samantha. How could a woman her age and with her beauty still be single?

Was she nursing a broken heart or was she too picky when it came to men? Not that it mattered one way or another. He didn't stand a chance with her. As much as he admired her beauty and determination he'd have to settle for fantasizing about the oil heiress.

"Can we do it, Dad?"

Luke's question snapped Wade out of his reverie. "Do what?"

"Dig a well." His son's expression mirrored both excitement and doubt.

"We'll give it our best shot." Wade didn't mind getting dirty or working up a sweat, but a handyman he was not. He'd grown up without a male role model to demonstrate how to pound a nail or measure and saw a board. When it had come to fixing a clogged sink or cleaning out the gutters Wade's uncle had hired a plumber or a yard service company.

The idea Wade might fail bothered him more than he cared to admit. He'd hate to embarrass himself in front of Sam again by bumbling the well-digging project— or worse, ending up in a predicament that required Samantha to rescue him.

"Miss Samantha's really pretty."

Had Luke guessed where his father's thoughts had drifted? "Yes, she is."

"And she's really nice."

Oh, boy. Luke was developing a crush on the cowgirl— another sign that his son needed more attention from Carmen. Wade suspected Luke would be thrilled if his father and Samantha dated. Wade might be tempted to test the waters with her if he wasn't already overcommitted— taking care of Luke more days than not while squeezing in sixty-hour work weeks. If those weren't good enough reasons to avoid a relationship with Samantha, then the firm losing her millions clinched the deal.

"She asked me what I liked most about school."

That must have been when Wade was busy arguing with Millicent over her dowsing abilities.

"I told her science." Luke flipped through the diagrams of well-digging equipment. "She said she used to like school, then it got too hard."

Hardly a surprise. Samantha had probably focused her time and energy on boys, parties and clothes rather than her studies.

"Dad?"

"What?"

"If you and Mom get married again we could all live in the same house."

Ah, damn. His son understood the meaning of divorce, but Luke continued to struggle with feelings of abandonment after Wade had moved out of the family home. Luke might have adjusted better if Carmen hadn't quit being a mother. Carmen's frequent overnight trips with various boyfriends before she'd become engaged again had reinforced the boy's feelings of insecurity. Carmen hadn't even tried to pretend Luke was her number one priority.

"Your mom and I are never getting back together but that doesn't mean we aren't still a family." Sort of.

"Are you gonna marry someone else?"

"Maybe, but I'm in no hurry." The notion of living alone the rest of his life didn't appeal to Wade and he hoped one day when Luke was older he'd fall in love with a nice woman and give marriage another try.

"Do you want more kids?"

"Heck no." Wade flashed a fake scowl. "You're too much trouble as it is."

"Yeah, right, Dad."

He ruffled his son's hair. "Why don't you head into the kitchen and see what we've got in the freezer for dinner. I need to make a quick call." As soon as Luke left the room, Wade dialed Samantha's cell phone number. He wanted to be sure she had no plans to back out of their well-digging deal.

"Hello?"

Wade cleared his throat. "Samantha, this is Wade Dawson."

"Hello, Wade."

The smoky sound of his name rolling off her tongue triggered a blip in his heartbeat.

"I apologize for disturbing you when you're busy with family and the wedding, but I wanted to assure you that I intend to show up at the Peterson property next Sunday to begin digging the well."

Silence—not even breath sounds on the other end of the line. "Samantha? Are you there?"

"Wade—"

His heart blipped faster.

"—I want to thank you for trying to save me money, but I've spoken with my brothers and they're recommending I call in professionals to dig the well."

Wade's heart skidded to a rubber-burning stop. "Let's see how much progress I make before we change plans?"

"I won't be able to drive out to the property Sunday. My father's planned a family breakfast before my brother and his wife leave on their honeymoon."

"No problem. Luke and I should be fine."

"Wade, you can't dig the well by yourself."

"Who says?" A bead of sweat rolled down his temple. "Luke and I have already done the research and it's a straightforward process." Feeling childish, he crossed his fingers behind his back.

"I'm not sure it's wise for Luke to be out there. I'd hate for him to get hurt." Samantha cared more about Luke's safety than Wade's ex-wife.

"The witch, I mean Millicent, will be around to keep an eye on Luke."

"Thanks just the same but—"

"Wait. Samantha, please don't back out. Luke and I have been looking forward to a father-son outing for a long time." If Wade crossed his fingers any tighter the skin on his knuckles would split open.

Silence.

"Luke's told a few friends about the project already and we purchased the tools and equipment earlier today." His damned fingers throbbed.

A sigh filtered through the connection. "All right, but if you run into problems—"

"We won't." Wade hoped the witch knew her stuff. "Enjoy the wedding festivities next weekend and I'll phone you Sunday evening with an update."

"Sure."

"Best wishes to the bride and groom." Wade hung up before Samantha had a chance to respond, fearing if their goodbye dragged on he'd sound desperate. He pried his fingers apart. All he had to do now was dig a sixty-foot hole in the ground by hand.

The way he figured, if he didn't hit water, he'd have already dug his own grave.

Chapter Five

Late Sunday morning Samantha parked her truck next to Wade's black BMW in front of the Peterson farmhouse. She'd intended to arrive earlier but Matt and Amy's send-off breakfast had lasted longer than expected. Then she'd twiddled her thumbs while her father had packed his bags for a business trip. Thank goodness Duke had offered to drive him to the ranch airstrip, freeing the way for Samantha to leave.

She drummed her fingers against the steering wheel. The tap, tap, tapping habit had developed in the later days of her recovery from brain surgery when impatience had outpaced progress. Sam closed her eyes and drew in deep, slow breaths. Doubts—the big scary kind—had increased in size and frequency since her visit to Dawson Investments over a week ago.

The small notebook tucked away in the glove compartment reminded her that she'd taken precautions in preparing for this venture. The day she'd contacted a Realtor she'd begun recording the date, time and topic of each meeting, phone call or discussion involving the purchase of the property. She'd done everything possible to guarantee the success of this project. Or had she?

Most days Sam ignored the insecurity that had become a part of her life since her accident sixteen years ago. The fact that this was the first time she'd embarked on a mission without the help of her brothers or father fueled her worry and confusion.

Had she made a mistake reaching for her own dream?

No. Have a little faith in yourself, Sam.

The past eight years she'd worked in her father's office she'd saved most of her salary and had used the money to purchase this homestead. Come hell or high water she'd open a sanctuary ranch and by doing so she'd learn to trust herself and gain the respect and confidence of others.

The memory of Bo's daughter was never far away. *Emily.* Sweet, innocent Emily had wandered off and gotten lost for hours because of Sam's absentmindedness. Sam couldn't change the past and as much as she'd love to be a mother she was better off sinking all her time and energy into saving horses.

Her thoughts shifted to Wade digging her well. *Good grief.* This was the twenty-first century. No one dug a well by hand—especially financial advisers. She doubted the man got his clothes dirty often. She could end all this nonsense by firing Wade as her financial adviser but she hated to disappoint Luke if the boy had his heart set on helping his father.

Her stomach churned with new worry—was there more behind digging the well than Wade let on? Instinct insisted he had her best interests at heart. But… *No buts.* Wade had given her no reason to believe he'd lead her astray.

Shoving the reservations to the back of her mind, she marched across the yard. When she rounded the corner of the barn she stopped and stared. So much for a father-son project. Luke sat on the ground beneath the hackberry tree reading to Millicent, who fumbled with a new pouch of tobacco. A Folgers coffee can rested in the dirt by her feet. Wade had paid Millicent for her water-witching services. His thoughtfulness warmed Sam's heart.

Wade stood with his back to her, wearing a long-sleeve sweat-soaked chambray shirt, jeans that hugged his academic butt and a pair of brand-new work boots. He glanced at the three-foot hole in the ground near his feet, shoved his glasses up his nose, then studied the piece of paper in his hand.

"Samantha," Luke called, when he noticed her. The boy scrambled to his feet and raced toward her. "Look at this. It's Millicent's family Bible and she said it belonged to her great-grandmother."

"That makes it really old." Sam glanced at Wade and noted his mouth hung open in surprise. Had he really expected her to stay away today?

"Yeah, like a hundred and ninety years." Luke pointed to the date written inside the Bible. "Eighteen-nineteen."

"Wow. That is old."

"Millicent's relatives are written here—" he flipped to the page of names scrawled in various people's hand-writing "—and it says who married who. See?" Luke's finger traced the faded print. "Millicent said her cousin Jack rode with Teddy Roosevelt and the Rough Riders."

"Stop pestering Samantha," Wade scolded when he joined her and Luke. "You're supposed to keep an eye on Millicent."

The boy rolled up on his tiptoes and whispered, "Dad says I have to stay with Millicent because she's too old to help and she'll get hurt." He skipped back to the tree.

"I thought Luke was eager to help dig the well." Sam studied Wade. For a geek, he was a handsome man— dusty face and all. Not even the mud marring his chin detracted from his strong jawline.

"Luke almost banged himself in the forehead when he stepped on the shovel head earlier this morning. Safer for both of us if he keeps out of the way."

Wade's words floated in one ear and out the other as Sam focused on the sweat beading across his forehead. A single droplet slid down his temple, curved inward across his cheek, skirted the corner of his mouth and dripped off his chin.

"Are you all right?" he asked.

His voice —or maybe his hand on her elbow—ended her trance. She shrugged off his touch, ignoring his raised eyebrow.

Wade cleared his throat. "I didn't expect to see you today."

"The wedding guests departed early." She motioned to the hole in the ground. "How's the digging coming along?"

His body tensed. "I was taking a short break."

At this pace he'd hit water around Christmas. Sam rolled up her sleeves. "I'll spell you."

"What?"

Were his ears clogged with dirt? "I'll dig for a while."

"I understand you want to get the ball rolling on this rescue ranch, but I don't think you should—"

"Shovel a little dirt?" A dusky hue seeped into his cheeks. Sam couldn't recall witnessing a man blush before and found the act charming. "Sorry to burst your bubble but I'm not a pampered princess."

The first month after she'd been discharged from the rehab hospital she'd had trouble concentrating for long periods of time, so she'd thrown herself into ranch chores because physical activity didn't tax her brain and leave her with a headache.

"This was my idea. I'll do the digging," he insisted.

Let him, a voice whispered inside her head. A man accustomed to sitting behind a desk all week wouldn't last a day toiling beneath the blazing Oklahoma sun. When he realized he was in over his head he'd give up and phone a contractor to dig the well, which had been her intent all along. She had two weeks—give or take a few days—until her father returned from Europe. The sooner Wade accepted defeat, the better. "Okay then. I'll leave you to the digging." She hadn't taken three steps when he called out.

"What are you going to do?"

"Decide where I want the paddocks." By the time Sam stopped at her truck she'd forgotten what she'd intended to get. She closed her eyes and forced herself to relax. The more she fretted the longer the duration of her memory lapse. Once her mind went blank she remembered the reason for going to the truck—her notepad. She removed the black notebook from the glove compartment and a pen from the cup holder, then wrote the word *Paddocks* on the paper.

Ignoring the sound of Wade's shovel scraping the ground, Sam studied the area adjacent to the house. Approximately thirty yards separated the soon-to-be paddocks from the well. A water pipe would need to be installed to carry well water to a spigot near the fenced-in area.

She spent the next half hour jotting down a list of fencing materials—hardware, posts, cement, water troughs, gate latches. Tomorrow she'd stop by Barney's Ranch Supply and order the items. She'd also ask Barney to spread the word that she needed a few hard-working cowboys—preferably not the nerdy kind—to install the fencing for the paddocks.

DAMN IT, SAMANTHA WASN'T supposed to show up today and witness him bumble his way through Well-Digging 101. The fact that Wade cared about her opinion of him caused concern. He might find her attractive, sexy and intriguing, but she was his client. If that wasn't enough of a reminder to keep things businesslike between them, then being held accountable for her lost trust fund should be.

He jumped on the edge of the shovel head with both feet and the tip sank deeper into the red clay. His arm muscles shook like Jell-O and his shoulders burned as if a hot branding iron had been pressed against his skin. A lot of good his three-a-week forty-minute workouts at the company health club did him.

You'd make more progress if you'd stop watching Samantha.

She sat on the rickety steps of the ranch house, doodling in a notebook. Once in a while she stared at the cloudless sky with a quizzical expression on her pretty face. Beauty aside, the woman confused the heck out of him. One minute she was a snippy miss know-it-all, the next she wore a lost-little-girl expression, which made Wade want to wrap his arms around her and protect her from the big bad bogeyman.

"Dad, I'm hungry." Luke's shadow fell over the hole.

Wade checked his watch. Noon. He and Luke had loaded a cooler with Gatorade bottles this morning but he hadn't thought to pack snacks or lunch food.

"That's not a very big hole." Luke glanced between the mound of dirt and the four-foot hole Wade stood at the bottom of.

Ignoring the criticism, Wade attempted to hoist himself out of the crater but his Jell-O arms wobbled and he slipped to the bottom, swallowing a groan as pain shot through his shoulders.

"Need a hand?" Samantha peered over the edge at him, fighting a smile.

What the hell. He'd already made an ass out of himself, he might as well accept her assistance. "Sure."

"On the count of three." She wrapped her fingers around his wrist. "One, two…three."

Wade scaled the side of the hole. When his hips cleared the edge, he flung himself forward and Samantha released her grip. "Thanks," he huffed, scrambling to his feet. For a pampered princess she had a heck of a grip.

"Next time put a ladder in the hole with ya," Millicent said, joining the group.

No kidding. The problem was he didn't have a ladder. "Luke and I are heading out for lunch." *And a ladder.*

"Where did you plan to eat?" Samantha asked.

"Nearest restaurant, I guess." Wade slapped at the dirt on his jeans.

"Ain't no nearest restaurant leastways ya mean Beulah's. She's closed on Sundays."

Great. Now what?

"Got me a kilt chicken," the old woman said. "An' fixins fer biscuits."

A *kilt* chicken? *Don't ask.*

"You two wash up. I'll help make lunch." Samantha and Millicent walked off.

"Where are we supposed to wash up?" Wade turned in a circle.

"Millicent said there's a little water left in the back-yard well." Luke pointed to the rundown farmhouse.

Wade followed his son, his arms flopping against his sides like overcooked noodles. He pumped the well handle twice.

Luke shoved a bucket under the small stream of water. "You're not supposed to waste any, Dad."

While Wade washed his hands in an inch of water, he contemplated jumping headfirst into the dark hole. His blistered fingers hurt. His sunburned neck itched. And his shoulders throbbed. What he wouldn't give for a long, cold shower.

"You're bleeding, Dad." Luke poked at an open blister on his father's palm.

"I'm fine." Next time he'd have to remember to bring along a pair of leather work gloves.

As soon as they entered Millicent's two-room shanty, Luke blurted, "My dad's hands are bleeding."

The old witch grunted an unintelligible word as she

flipped pieces of chicken in a skillet of hot grease. Samantha, bless her sympathetic heart, didn't ignore him. She turned his hands palm side up. "Ouch."

What did she mean, *ouch?* He couldn't feel a thing except for the tingling sensation that followed in the wake of her finger as she caressed the raw flesh around each blister.

"Sit," she commanded.

Feeling light-headed, Wade collapsed onto one of the ladder-back chairs at the crudely made table, which sat in the center of the cabin. Samantha brought a shoebox filled with jars and strips of clean cloth to the table. "Let's see what Millicent has in her first aid kit."

Wade eyed the collection of small jars but didn't recognize any products commonly found in a drugstore. Samantha must have read his mind, because she smiled reassuringly as she spread a salve that smelled like a dead animal carcass across his wounds.

"You should stop digging, Wade. These sores will take days to heal."

His name slipped from her mouth in a gentle rush of air that soughed across his palm. He wanted to take her advice but calling it quits for the day wasn't possible—not unless he intended to tell her the truth right here and now. *Samantha, you're broke. That's why I'm making a fool of myself.* "A couple of Band-Aids and my hands will be good as new."

"Don't be silly."

Silly? He yearned to confess the well-digging fiasco had been a stall tactic to prevent her from spending money she didn't have. Money he had to front her from his personal funds. Instead he had to act *silly* and insist he didn't mind digging a frickin' hole in the ground with blistered hands.

Samantha returned the shoebox to the shelf next to the ancient cast-iron sink. "Tomorrow I'll contact a drilling company and offer a financial incentive to dig sooner rather than later. While we wait on the permits, I'll hire a crew to fence in the paddocks."

"Give me a week, Samantha, and I'll have the hole dug." Grasping at straws, he added, "Your father will be impressed by how frugal you were with your inheritance."

A wrinkle formed across her brow and Wade curled his stinging hand into a fist to keep from caressing her forehead and discovering if her skin felt as velvety as it appeared.

"Maybe you're right." She sat across the table from him. "In any regard your hands have seen enough work for one day."

"I can help," Luke offered, carrying a stack of plates to the table.

Samantha smiled at his son and Wade swore Luke stood a few inches taller. "We'll both take turns," she said.

Damned if he'd allow a woman to show him up. "No need to ruin your hands, too," he argued.

"You really don't believe I'm capable of shoveling a little dirt?" Her eyes gleamed with challenge.

"I doubt you've done much work—" *Damn.* He should have kept his mouth shut.

Face red with anger, Samantha nodded at his bandaged hands. "You're one to talk."

True.

"How about a wager?" she said, winking at his son. "Luke and I will dig three more feet by suppertime."

Great. First Samantha had shown him up with her tree-climbing talents and now she was about to defeat him in a well-digging competition. Couldn't a hard-working investor get a break?

Blast, it was hot.

Samantha was ringing wet, her shirt soaked with sweat and plastered to her skin. Wade's son was just as exhausted, but the sweet boy hadn't uttered one word of complaint. Sam rested against the old ladder she'd found in the barn and handed the bucket of dirt to Luke, which he dumped a few feet away.

They'd made decent progress, but her arms were sore and her shoulders itched from the dirt that had slipped inside her collar when Luke had accidentally tipped a full bucket onto Sam's back.

"Looking good, Samantha," Wade complimented for the hundredth time. She wished he'd stop hovering and go chew tobacco with Millicent.

Sam feared her plan might backfire. She'd insisted on taking a turn at digging because she'd hoped to guilt Wade into agreeing to call in the professionals to finish the well. Most men would have felt compassion for a struggling woman. As a matter of fact the cowboys she knew would have insisted she quit shoveling hours ago. Obviously financial advisers had no problem with women showing them up.

Needing a break she set aside the short-handled

shovel and climbed from the hole. Without warning Wade removed her gloves and checked her hands.

"No blisters?" He sounded disappointed.

Sam shook off his touch. "Unlike you, my fingers rarely spend time on a keyboard."

Wade's shoulders stiffened and a businesslike mask fell over his face. "Luke, fetch Ms. Cartwright a drink from the cooler." As soon as his son ran off, Wade glanced into the hole. "You made good progress. I'd say it's about six feet."

From disappointment to admiration—Wade confused the heck out of her. Luke arrived with Gatorade bottles and they took a break from conversation to quench their thirst. Sam's eyes strayed to Wade's Adam's apple, which bobbed up and down as he swallowed. A vision of her tongue tracing the sexy bump popped into her mind and she choked.

Wade slapped her back. "Down the wrong pipe?"

Nodding, she coughed again and wiped her watering eyes. For the hundredth time that day Wade pushed his glasses up his nose. "Why don't you wear contacts?" She blurted the question that had been on her mind since meeting him.

"Contacts irritate my eyes."

"Maybe you should consider laser eye surgery." Didn't he hate having to adjust his glasses all the time?

"Dad says our glasses are a sign of intelligence and we should be proud to wear them." Luke gazed up at his father. "Right, Dad?"

Oh, dear. She hadn't meant to wound their egos.

"Break's over," Wade announced. "Back to digging."

She'd heard once that high-IQ people lacked common sense and wondered if Wade fell into that category. One thing was clear—even if her arms transformed into rotary blades, they wouldn't hit water today. She might as well put an end to this nonsense. "I'm quitting," she announced.

Both males gaped at her. "What about the bet?" Luke asked.

"Your dad wins." That ought to make up for any bruised feelings from her four-eyes comment.

The corner of Wade's mouth lifted in a sexy half smile. "What's my prize?"

"Your prize is that you don't have to shovel anymore. I'm calling a drilling company tomorrow and that's final."

"But—"

"No buts, Wade. This is my project. My money. And we're doing this my way." She stomped off, forcing her legs to keep moving when Wade called her name.

"Wait, Samantha!" Footsteps pounded the earth behind her.

She'd made it to her truck when Wade stumbled to a halt. "Luke wants to keep digging the well. He's having a great time. Please give us a week. If we don't hit water, I'll step aside and we'll do this your way."

Luke caught up to them and both males gazed at her through their eyeglasses. How was she supposed to resist such a cute pair of geeks?

"Okay. You've got until next Sunday. Then all bets are off."

Chapter Six

"Find anything yet?" Wade asked George, the systems analyst called in to search the company's software program for Samantha's missing trust fund.

Fingers clicking the keyboard at hyperspeed, the balding man in his late fifties grunted an unintelligible answer.

Wade moved to the office doorway and stared at the empty conference rooms across the hall. Due to his uncle's extended absence, the firm's senior executives were conducting business meetings on the golf course while employees on the lower rungs of the company ladder managed to squeeze in online shopping, long-distance calls to family and friends and two-hour lunches.

Wasting company time was the least of Wade's worries. He flexed his stiff fingers. His stint as a weekend cowboy had taken a toll on his body. Monday night he'd caved in and paid for a massage at the gym. Tuesday he'd sat for a half hour in the whirlpool and made another appointment with Helga and her meat-grinding fingers. Wednesday he weaned himself off the Icy Hot patches and this morning he was able to roll out of bed without wincing—just in time for another round of abuse this weekend.

Ignoring the queasy feeling that had plagued his stomach all week, he shoved his hands deep into his trouser pockets and rocked back on his wing tips. Even if he succeeded in digging the sixty-foot well by Sunday evening, he doubted Samantha would approve of him shoveling the trenches to lay water pipe from the well to the paddocks.

"Sir."

"What is it?" Wade bolted to his desk and peered over George's shoulder at the jumbled symbols, letters and numbers on the computer screen.

"These codes—" George pointed to the top of the screen "—verify that the account in question was accessed by an unknown user."

"A computer hacker?"

George shrugged. "The user ID isn't registered to anyone in the company." He tapped a series of numbers. "And this code tells me that the transaction wasn't made on your computer."

"If not mine, then whose?"

"Computer 12785." George ran a finger between his neck and the collar of his tight shirt. "That computer is registered to your uncle, sir."

Absurd! His uncle wouldn't steal from his own company. Someone must have had access to his uncle's computer. "Is there an exact time and date the funds were withdrawn?"

"July fourth at two-fifteen in the afternoon."

Wade had attended the Tulsa parade with Luke in the morning that day and later in the afternoon they'd stopped by his uncle's for the annual Dawson Investments barbecue. Wade couldn't recall if all the VPs had shown up for the event. Not that it mattered. Anyone could have slipped away for an hour or two unnoticed. Wade would need to view the building's security tapes for that day.

George checked his watch. "I'm meeting my wife for lunch. Is there anything else, sir?"

"No. Thanks for coming in today."

"I hope you find the culprit who tampered with the account."

"Keep this between you and me for a while, all right, George?"

"Sure."

Left alone, Wade returned to his desk and buzzed the receptionist.

"Yes, Mr. Dawson?"

"Veronica, get me the number of the company that operates the security cameras in the building."

"Right away, sir."

While he waited for the information, Wade paced his office, his thoughts straying to Samantha. His ego wished to impress her—change her opinion of him. He admitted he wasn't the kind of man a woman like her would give a second thought. He didn't walk with a swagger. Didn't possess bulging biceps. Wasn't tall— Samantha darn near looked him in the eye.

And he wore glasses.

Why don't you wear contact lenses?

Deep in his gut he believed Samantha's question hadn't been meant as a criticism. He'd sounded like an idiot when he'd explained that contacts dried his eyes out. He'd considered laser eye surgery—had even scheduled a consultation appointment with a doctor over a year ago, but he'd chickened out at the last minute.

And you know why.

Wade attempted to block out the annoying voice in his head, but the nasty bugger refused to be subdued.

Because you hide behind your glasses.

That's insane.

Or was it?

Few were aware that Wade's business smarts hadn't come easy.

Not until the third grade had his dyslexia been diagnosed. Once he'd been given the tools to overcome his reading challenges he'd embraced learning, but had continued to struggle to keep pace with the rest of his classmates. Then his mother had died and his uncle had taken him in and insisted he attend a prestigious allboys school. If not for a sympathetic instructor who'd tutored him, Wade would have flunked out of the academy. The grade reports he'd brought home had been nothing short of a miracle. Only the fear of disappointing his uncle prevented Wade from conceding defeat.

The battle continued in college. His uncle's promise of a job at Dawson Investments upon graduation had motivated Wade to sacrifice friends, sports and a social life. He'd graduated near the top of his business class, then had been hired by Dawson Investments and handed Samantha's trust fund to manage. Wade had believed his promotion to VP was a slam dunk—until this latest fiasco.

What if his uncle was involved in the disappearance of Samantha's funds? He shoved the thought aside.

He'd view the security tapes before jumping to conclusions.

Samantha won't criticize you if you take off your glasses.

How did he know? Because she intended to care for unwanted horses? Because she treated Luke kindly, had taken an old woman under her wing and had appeared genuinely concerned about his blistered hands? *None of that means the pampered princess isn't above putting you in your place.*

Samantha flustered him. She was friendly and approachable yet aloof and guarded. One minute she acted self-confident and downright bossy. The next uncertain. Her *uncertain* moments tugged at Wade's heartstrings and he yearned to please her, slay her dragons, right her wrongs—basically make an ass of himself around her.

He knew one thing for sure—he'd never have a shot at being her hero if he didn't recover her money.

WHAT THE HELL WAS GOING ON?

Since Wade wouldn't receive copies of the company security tapes until next week he'd decided to skip work Friday and head out to the Peterson homestead, hoping to make progress on the well-digging before Samantha showed up tomorrow morning. He hadn't expected to find a dozen half-naked cowboys strutting around the place.

Wade slowed his car to a stop and stared at the assortment of pickups parked near the farmhouse. Where was Samantha? He spotted her writing in her trusty notebook while a cowboy—a tall, muscular, no-eye-glasses kind of cowboy—talked her ear off.

The guy's words must have tickled her funny bone, because Samantha's head fell back and she laughed. Her full-blown smile caught Wade in the gut, stealing his breath. What he wouldn't give to make her laugh that hard.

Feeling like a misfit among a gathering of Marlboro men, Wade shoved his glasses up his nose and got out of the car. He made a beeline for the barn, hoping his presence would go unnoticed. Fat chance.

Each cowboy Wade strolled by stopped. Turned. Stared. Twenty steps later Samantha's voice smacked him in the back of the head.

"Wade!"

Crap. He waited for her to catch up with him, hoping she wouldn't make a big deal of his presence in front of the work crew. Face smudged with dirt and her braid unraveling, she'd never looked sexier.

"What are you doing here? Weren't we supposed to meet tomorrow morning?"

"Things were slow at work this week so I decided to take today off and put in a few hours digging the well." He knew how badly she wanted the project finished by Sunday night. There wasn't a chance in hell of making that deadline, but he was determined to give it his best shot.

Instead of appearing pleased, she scowled. "You should have called me."

He nodded toward the others. "If you're worried I'll get in the way—"

"I would have told you not to bother showing up today. Or any other day."

"Why?"

"The guys offered to finish digging the well." She motioned to the milling cowboys.

Wade stared at the throng of sweaty musclemen and clenched his jaw. The walls were closing in on him and damned if he could find an escape route.

"I appreciate that you're trying to save me money, Wade, but there's no reason to wear yourself out—"

Was she implying that he was a wuss?

"—when I have the funds to pay professionals to dig a well."

"And these cowboys are professional well-diggers?"

"No. They're my brother's rodeo friends. But most of them have grown up on ranches and have construction experience."

Wade's gaze took in the workmen and he conceded that they did indeed appear qualified to dig wells and install fences. "How are you paying for supplies?" He motioned to the wooden posts the cowboys were unloading from the pickups.

"I charged the materials to my account at Barney's Ranch Supply."

Wade swallowed the knot in his throat. "How much did you spend?"

"Aside from the fencing, I ordered two water tanks, feeding bins and a few other items. Came to a little over six thousand dollars."

"What are you paying these guys to help out?"

"Nothing. Juanita, my father's housekeeper, is making her famous barbecue pork sandwiches for the men. You're welcome to join us when we finish for the day."

He'd stand out like a sore thumb among the ropers.

"Thanks for the invite, but Luke's mother is dropping him off at my condo tonight." He hated asking but his bruised male ego lashed out. "Do all these guys live around here?"

"No. The rodeo's in town this weekend." She chuckled. "Cowboys will do anything for a home-cooked meal."

A home-cooked meal and a beautiful woman. "When do we owe Barney's Ranch Supply a payment on your account?"

"Barney sends out a bill once a month."

At least Wade had enough in his savings account to pay off the fencing costs without dipping into his 401(k). "I'd better get to work." He walked away, expecting her to call him back, praying she wouldn't.

She didn't.

Wade shimmied down the ladder and slowly chipped away at the ground with the short-handled shovel until he'd filled the bucket with dirt. Then he hauled the bucket up the ladder, tossed the dirt out and began the process all over again.

"Yer gonna get mighty tuckered climbin' up 'n down all day." Millicent flashed a toothless smile when Wade poked his head out of the hole. Knobby hands set a water jug on the ground. "Where's that youngin' o' yers?"

"My sidekick is in summer school today. He'll be here tomorrow." Wade dumped the bucket of dirt, careful to avoid the old woman's shoes. "Thanks for the drink."

Millicent puckered her mouth. "Why don't ya let them cowboys finish diggin' the well? Go a lot faster."

Because, damn it. He intended to prove that he could

pull his weight as well as any cowboy. Wade didn't care to delve too deeply into his reasons for needing to impress Samantha. He'd rather believe guilt urged him to continue shoveling dirt. Samantha's father had entrusted his daughter's money to Dawson Investments and they'd screwed up. "Isn't it time for your nap?" he asked the old biddy.

"Watch yer britches, young feller, lest I put a hex on ya." Millicent hobbled over to the rocking chair, sat and stared daggers at Wade.

Great. Not only was he being shown up by a bunch of cowboys, but a water witch threatened to cast a spell on him. Wade descended to the bottom of the hole, figuring he didn't need anyone's help digging his own path to hell.

"WANT US TO RESCUE HIM?"

Sam spun at the sound of the gravelly voice. "What?" she asked Connor, one of her brother's rodeo buddies.

He motioned to the hole in the ground fifty yards away. "You've been staring in his direction for the past two hours—" he shrugged a pair of wide shoulders "—figured you had the hots for the guy."

Connor believed she lusted after Wade? "Wade Dawson is my financial adviser. He's trying to save me money digging the well by hand."

"Like hell you say?" Connor grinned until the corners of his mouth threatened to split.

Sam giggled. "Nope."

"I'll be damned." The cowboy frowned. "You're sure he's not after a share of the Cartwright fortune for himself?"

"His uncle owns Dawson Investments in Tulsa. Wade pulls in a healthy income." She doubted he had millions like her but he drove a nice car and she'd noticed the quality of his suits and shirts. The executive had no trouble making ends meet.

Right then Wade's head popped out of the hole. He flung the bucket toward the pile nearby, but the afternoon winds blew half the dirt back in his face. Maybe the poor man did need to be rescued. Pride was well and good until stubbornness impeded progress. "Let him be for a while longer."

"Whatever you say, boss." Connor touched his fingers to the brim of his hat. "Larry's bringing in the water tanker. We'll be ready to mix the cement and set the posts shortly."

"Holler if you need any help," she said.

As soon as the cowboy walked off, Sam's thoughts returned to Wade. Did he really want to save her money or was there another reason Wade was killing himself?

Maybe he's trying to impress you.

The possibility sparked a tingle in her toes that worked its way up her calf, zipped through her thigh and migrated into her stomach. She couldn't compete intellectually with Wade—of that she was certain. So what did he see in her that made him want to prove he wasn't afraid of hard work or getting his hands dirty?

Too much pondering gave her a headache. "Hold up, Jake!" She jogged over to an empty wheelbarrow, then steered the contraption toward the cowboy who'd been wrestling with two bags of cement. "Use this."

"Thanks, Sam." Jake loaded the bags into the wheelbarrow and went on his way.

Now why couldn't Wade be as cooperative? Seeing there wasn't much else for her to do while the men cemented the posts into the ground, she checked on Millicent.

"The man's dumber 'n a doorknob," the old woman said as soon as Sam sat on a patch of dirt next to the rocking chair. "Told 'im to let the others dig the well, but he—"

"Said he didn't need help," Sam finished.

Millicent spit a stream of tobacco juice at the dirt. "Stubborn as a mule."

Wade wasn't the only obstinate person in the bunch. When Sam had visited the Peterson homestead with her Realtor they'd both been surprised to discover Millicent living in a cabin on the property. The Realtor had suggested Sam contact the sheriff's department and have Millicent forcibly removed, but Sam hadn't had the heart. If she intended to provide a sanctuary for unwanted horses she couldn't turn her back on a lonely old woman with nowhere to go.

Sam had returned to the property a few days later without the Realtor and visited with Millicent. The old woman had explained that the Dust Bowl years and the Depression had forced the Petersons to sell off large parcels of land and turn the farm into a small cattle ranch. Millicent's father had helped with the herd while her mother had done the laundry, cooking and cleaning.

When Millicent turned seventeen she'd met an army soldier at a local dance and, shortly after, they'd married and moved in with his family in Arkansas. World War II broke out and Millicent's husband had been shipped overseas. Millicent gave birth to a baby boy a week before she'd received the news that her young husband had died in action. So she'd gathered her belongings and the baby and had returned to the Petersons.

Millicent never remarried. She'd spent her days taking care of her aging parents and helping Mrs. Peterson with household chores. Time passed and Millicent's son had dropped out of school and left for California. He'd returned twice through the years to visit his mother, but Millicent confessed she hadn't heard from him in two decades. Odds were her son wasn't alive anymore. Eventually Millicent's parents and the Petersons had passed away, leaving Millicent alone on the property.

When Sam had assured Millicent she'd always have a home on the ranch, the old woman had teared up and offered to clean and cook for Sam once she built a new house on the property. Sam understood the need to feel useful only too well, so she'd agreed to Millicent's offer.

"He ain't half-bad ta look at," the old woman said.

"No, he's not." Wade was definitely an attractive man—in a studious kind of way. She switched her attention to the cowboys heckling each other as they wrestled with the fence posts. Rodeo cowboys were full of muscle, bravado, bragging and mischief. They lived and breathed danger. Risked their lives on the backs of rank broncs or raging bulls. For years Sam had believed a rodeo cowboy was exactly the kind of man she wanted. Admired. Desired.

But she no longer envisioned herself spending the rest of her life with a rough-'n-ready cowboy. She needed a man who calmed and soothed her anxious spirit. A patient man who didn't mind repeating things.

A man who tolerated her memory lapses. A man who loved her despite her shortcomings.

And a man who didn't have or want children.

Wade emerged from the hole with another bucket of dirt. Her heart sighed. He was the furthest thing from a real cowboy she'd ever met, yet he risked making a fool of himself to save a wealthy woman money. If only he wasn't a father already, Sam would be tempted to test the relationship waters again with Wade.

Uh, oh.

Connor stopped at the well and spoke to Wade.

Sam was too far away to catch the discussion, but Wade's frown told her he took exception to whatever the cowboy had said. Right then a group of wranglers joined Connor, brushing Wade aside. In a frenzy of activity, the men constructed a pulley system to lower and raise the bucket of dirt. Wade was pushed farther and farther from the group as the cowboys shouted bets on who could dig faster.

Sam got to her feet, intending to intervene when Wade whipped off his shirt and shoved his way back into the fray. The look of determination on his face snatched Sam's breath. Even the cowboys understood Wade wouldn't be deterred from helping. Pride swelled in her chest. Her financial adviser didn't need anyone to fight his battles for him.

"Suppose we gotta fix some vittles fer the men," Millicent said.

"Don't bother. They're all heading to the Lazy River for a barbecue. Juanita's been cooking since yesterday. Care to join us?" Millicent hadn't socialized with people in years and Sam doubted she'd begin today.

"Well, now that would be nice but I gotta mess of things needin' my attention. Best I get to 'em." Millicent pushed herself out of the chair and wobbled toward her cabin.

Time passed slowly as Sam watched Wade—more specifically his chest. For a guy who wore a suit to work he had nicely defined pecs and biceps. Not the bulging muscles the cowboys flaunted but the lean, hard muscles of a swimmer or a runner. Sam studied the intriguing patch of dark hair in the middle of his chest, before following the line of fuzz down his stomach, where it disappeared beneath the waistband of his Wranglers. When her eyes reversed direction, she discovered Wade staring at her.

Their gazes clashed and Wade's brown eyes smoldered with invitation.

Oh, boy. She was in trouble.

Big trouble.

Chapter Seven

A caravan of pickup trucks departed from the ranch, leaving a cloud of dust hanging in the air. Sam peeked at Wade and the intensity of his brown-eyed stare sent a jolt through her. Suddenly she didn't want to say goodbye. "You're coming to the Lazy River for barbecue, aren't you?"

"I've got Luke this weekend."

At the risk of sounding eager for his attention, she suggested, "Could Luke's mom drop him off later in the evening?"

Wade's gaze slipped to her mouth. "Maybe."

Maybe what? Maybe he'd come to the barbecue? Or maybe he'd kiss her? Feeling short of breath she said, "I'll wait in my truck." As soon as she got inside the cab she watched Wade in the rearview mirror, wondering how friendly he and his ex-wife were.

Questions like… Whose idea had the divorce been— the ex's or Wade's? Did Wade still love the woman? Had infidelity played a role in their breakup? Wade didn't act like the cheating kind. Then again, where men were concerned, Sam's judgment had failed her before.

Sam had believed Bo would forgive her for accidentally putting his daughter in danger. Never in Sam's wildest dreams had she expected he'd quit their relationship out of fear for Emily's safety.

Wade's expression remained neutral while talking on the phone, then he turned away and Sam worried the conversation had taken a nosedive. She prepared herself for disappointment as he drew near and leaned his head inside the truck window. "Carmen agreed to bring Luke by my place tomorrow morning."

The scent of his faded cologne filled the cab and for a split second Sam lost her train of thought. "Great." His mouth was so close if she leaned a little to the left... Wade stepped back and cleared his throat. *Oh, God.* Had she almost kissed him? What was she thinking? "Follow me." She raised the window and flipped the air conditioner to high while Wade got into his car.

Okay, she was attracted to Wade and she wanted to kiss him. There. She admitted it. Now what?

Nothing. She shifted into Drive and headed to the county road, Wade's Beamer eating her dust. There could be no future for her and Wade because of Luke, and a sixth sense insisted Wade didn't do flings. Shoot, she didn't do flings.

Once the truck tires hit pavement Sam increased her speed. She glanced in the rearview mirror and noticed the Beamer growing smaller. She checked the speedometer, then yanked her foot from the gas pedal. Eighty was a bit too fast even for a rural road.

There was nothing left for her and Wade but friendship, which stunk. The more she saw of Wade Dawson the more of him she wanted. He was different from the men in her past—less intimidating. His quiet stares and calm demeanor tempted her to believe she could trust him not to use her weaknesses against her. And she admitted that she was developing a soft spot for those goofy glasses he wore. Not to mention she found Wade flat-out sexy.

Sam's pulse jumped as her mind conjured up an image of Wade's toned chest. Unlike the other cowboys who tripped over their muscles, Wade's body moved in a smooth, stealthy manner and she suspected his talent in bed was skillful and practiced.

Four years after her accident Sam had succumbed to the flowery speech of a cowboy and had ended up sharing his saddle blanket—big mistake. Her memory had failed her the following morning when she'd awoken in a panic next to the naked man. Not until Bo had come along a few years later had Sam been ready to test the waters again. This time she'd been honest with Bo from the onset and had explained her accident and its lingering effects on her memory.

Bo had been supportive and understanding and hadn't pressured her into a physical relationship. Eventually their friendship advanced to the bedroom, but sex had been awkward. Bo had acted tense and uncertain—as if he'd expected Sam to suffer a nervous breakdown in his arms. Before they'd had a chance to work out the kinks in their lovemaking, she'd botched things with Emily and Bo had ended the relationship.

Making love with Wade would be different. Better.

Whoa! Aren't you jumping the gun? He hasn't even kissed you.

Sam responded to Wade in a way she hadn't with

other men. He tempted her to let down her guard—maybe because she'd witnessed a vulnerability in him that matched her own. Regardless of why she was drawn to him she believed their lovemaking would be an experience she'd remember forever.

Forever? You can't recall one day from the next.

Today she'd noticed that she hadn't worried over her forgetfulness. Hadn't feared repeating herself or asking the same question more than once. Miraculously she hadn't felt the need to hide her shortcomings. The thought was both joyous and sad. Why did the one man she could see herself taking a chance on have to be a father?

She hated admitting she was jealous of her brothers, Duke and Matt. Both had found their own happy-ever-after with the woman of their dreams. And both were fathers. Sam wanted at least half that dream—a man of her own to love and grow old with. She ached to be a mother, to experience the special bond between mother and child but the risks were too great. She'd have to settle for enjoying the time she had with Wade.

Forty minutes had passed when Sam parked in front of the main house on the Lazy River Ranch. Wade pulled alongside her truck. Neither spoke as they climbed the porch steps at the side of the house.

"I'd like to wash up," he said when they stepped into the kitchen.

"Sure." The raucous laughter of cowboys splashing in the pool filtered through the screen door that led outside to the patio.

"Juanita," Sam said when the housekeeper entered the room. "Meet Wade Dawson. He's helping me with the Peterson homestead." She'd sworn Juanita to secrecy about the horse sanctuary. If she didn't confess her whereabouts every day the housekeeper would send the state patrol searching for Sam.

"Pleasure meeting you, Juanita. I hear your barbecue is famous."

"There's plenty, *señor.*"

"Bathroom's down the hallway on the right." Sam pointed to the doorway.

As soon as Wade disappeared, Juanita elbowed Sam in the side. "He's handsome, no?"

"He's also nice." Sam washed up at the kitchen sink. "I like him a lot."

"Be yourself, *mi pequeña querida.*" Juanita wrapped an arm around Sam's waist.

Wade returned to the kitchen—hair slicked back with water, the wet strands transforming the geek into a bad boy. "The house looks the same as I remembered," he said, pushing his glasses up his nose.

Had Wade visited the ranch before? Oh, God, Sam couldn't remember. Her breath burning in her lungs, she glanced at Juanita. Where was all her newfound confidence now?

"Ah, I remember you, *señor.*" Juanita clasped Sam's hand. "You were the young man who fell from the tree and broke your arm years ago."

The air in Sam's lungs escaped in a loud whoosh. Wade had mentioned the tree-climbing incident when they'd first met at Dawson Investments and again at the Peterson property. Why did she keep forgetting?

"I'm afraid I didn't make much of an impression on Samantha." Wade grinned. "She doesn't recall that day."

Juanita waved her hand. "Sam cares only about horses. Horses this, horses that."

Grateful for the housekeeper's support, Sam joked, "Horses are smarter than men."

Wade chuckled, his eyes shifting nervously about the room. That he was uneasy calmed Sam's nerves. "I'm starving. Let's sample the barbecue." She led the way to the outdoor patio. The cowboys shouted greetings and a few called Wade by name. Pleased that her brother's friends had made Wade feel welcome, she said, "Drinks are this way." They stopped in front of a wheelbarrow filled with ice and cold beverages. Sam chose a diet soda and Wade selected a beer.

"For a greenhorn you did a good job today." Connor helped himself to a beer. The cowboy was one of a handful of Matt's friends who knew how severe Sam's head injury had been. She appreciated his big-brother concern but suspected he'd hover over her until he was convinced Wade meant no harm.

"If you'll excuse me for a minute." Sam walked off to thank the others for their help, leaving Wade at the mercy of Connor. If the cowboy's interrogation didn't send him running, then that would add more proof that Wade was as special as she believed.

Wade resisted the urge to call Samantha back to his side as he faced off with the cowboy.

"Sam's never mentioned you before." Connor rubbed the perspiring longneck against his forehead.

"She's never mentioned you, either." Why the hell had Wade gone and said that? He acted as if he was staking a claim on Samantha. *Aren't you?*

"Are you and Samantha a couple?"

Yes. "No." *Maybe.* Wade guzzled his beer. The alcohol fed his courage. "What about you?"

"What about me?"

"Are you and Samantha…"

Connor's laughter drew stares, including Samantha's from the other side of the pool. "Hardly. I'm her adopted big brother."

A sudden spell of light-headedness hit Wade and he blamed the feeling on the beer and not the relief he felt at the cowboy's declaration.

"Matt and I traveled the circuit together," Connor continued. "Matt was considered one of the top ten tie-down ropers the past few years. I bust broncs."

"Matt's the brother who recently married?"

"Yep. Went and tied the matrimonial noose around his neck."

Wade grinned. "You've never been married."

"Nope. And I'm not looking to walk down the aisle anytime soon."

"I'm divorced," Wade said. "I have an eight-year-old son."

"Can't remember Sam ever dating a married man."

"I'm not married." Was the guy hard of hearing? "And Samantha and I aren't dating. We're…" he hesitated "…friends."

"Sam said you were her accountant."

"Financial adviser." Accountants were dweebs. Wade wasn't a dweeb.

"Then you're aware she's worth a fortune."

A fortune Wade had worked tirelessly to expand over the past few years. "Her trust fund is in good hands." He hoped his expression didn't expose the lie.

"Glad to hear that." One of the men in the pool hollered for Connor to join their water basketball game. "If you hurt her—" the cowboy invaded Wade's space "—I'll stomp you flatter than a bull's hoof. Are we clear?"

"Crystal."

Connor set his beer on a table, whipped off his shirt, then did a canonball into the pool next to Wade, drenching him.

Asshole. Wade removed his eyeglasses and used the backside of his shirt to dry the lenses.

Ignoring the Neanderthals in the pool, he joined Samantha and an elderly Hispanic man. Her eyes widened at his soaked clothes. He offered his hand to the older gentleman. "I'm Wade Dawson, Samantha's financial investor."

"Armando Garcia."

"Armando is Juanita's husband. He takes care of the pool and the grounds," Samantha added.

"I've heard your wife's barbecue pork is the best this side of the Red River."

Armando grinned. *"Sí, señor."*

"Hungry, Samantha?" Wade wanted to whisk her away from the buffoons at the party.

"Starved." They headed to the buffet table, where they loaded their plates with meat, beans and potato salad.

"Why don't we eat on the front porch," Wade suggested, having remembered seeing a hanging swing when they'd arrived. They strolled to the front of the house, then climbed the porch steps and sat on the swing. After his first bite he moaned. "This is unbelievable."

"Told you so." Samantha winked. A cute, sassy blink of the eye that stole Wade's breath.

He ate another bite of pork and chewed slowly until his heart rate slowed to normal. "How long has Juanita worked for your family?"

"Since my mother ran away."

"Didn't your mother die in a car accident a few years ago?" His uncle and aunt had attended the funeral.

"That was Laura. My stepmother. Duke's mom."

"I'm sorry." All this time Wade had believed Matt and Duke were Samantha's biological brothers.

"My real mother took off when Matt and I were toddlers. I don't remember her at all." Samantha stared into space, her food forgotten.

Time to change the subject even if his admission bordered on unprofessional, considering Sam was his client. "You were the most beautiful girl I'd ever seen."

Startled, she gaped. At least his declaration had erased the desolate look in her eyes. "The afternoon I visited the ranch with my uncle you wore your hair loose, the strands falling down your back like a silky waterfall… And then you opened your mouth and cursed me."

Samantha's face flushed.

"I suppose you don't remember that, either." He chuckled. "I should have confessed that I'd never climbed a tree before, but I refused to be shown up by a girl."

"I won't believe you if you tell me you didn't have a tree to play in when you were a kid." Samantha quirked an eyebrow.

Wade rarely spoke about his childhood—not even Carmen had been interested in Wade's life before his uncle had taken him in. "It's a long story."

"I'm in no hurry." The honesty in her gaze assured him that she wouldn't judge his mother harshly.

The Samantha sitting next to him on the swing was such a contrast to the young woman he'd met years ago. The old Samantha wouldn't have cared about anyone but herself.

"My mother was Uncle Charles's younger sister and she was a rebel. She fell in love with a guy who rode into town on a Harley. He took off at the end of the summer, leaving my mother behind. When she discovered she was pregnant with me she left town in search of my father."

"Did she ever find him?"

"Nope. We were on the move, living in motel rooms, apartments and city shelters until I turned five." He had few memories of those years—probably a good thing. We stopped looking for my father when I entered kindergarten." The school district had forced Wade's mother to take him to a medical clinic for vaccinations before allowing him to attend school. His arms had been sore for a week afterward.

"Did your mother ever marry?"

"No." Wade believed his mother had loved his father even as she took her last breath. "She died of cancer when I was ten."

"Oh, Wade. I'm sorry."

"When she was diagnosed with pancreatic cancer and learned she had only a few months to live, we returned to Tulsa and she asked my uncle to raise me."

"Where were your grandparents?"

"They'd passed away years earlier."

"Was it difficult adjusting to a new family?"

"Yes." His aunt and uncle had afforded Wade little time to mourn his mother before they'd demanded nothing less than his best behavior and effort in school. "My uncle enrolled me and my cousin in a boys' private school, and I worked hard to earn good grades."

Samantha nudged his side with her elbow and smiled. "So the glasses are just for show? You aren't a brainiac?"

"I inherited bad eyesight but not a high IQ." Wade suspected his birth father had possessed more charm than intellect. "My son inherited the genius gene from Carmen's side of the family." Her brother was a physicist, the other a bio-medical engineer and her mother had been a concert pianist. Carmen was a smart woman but preferred shopping and socializing to using her brains. "Luke amazes me. He's a walking encyclopedia with a photographic memory."

They ate in silence for a minute, then Wade said, "To make a long story short, I studied and earned good grades because I wanted to make my mother proud of me." At least Wade had begun with that mindset. As years passed, pleasing his deceased mother had shifted to earning his uncle's respect and securing a foothold in Dawson Investments.

"How about your cousin. Is he an investor, too?" Samantha asked.

"Jarrod's a dentist. He lives in California with his life partner, Richard."

"I see."

"Jarrod calls around the holidays but his relationship with my aunt and uncle is strained."

"That's too bad."

Wade agreed. His mother's death had driven home the point that life was too short to allow rifts to grow between family members. His uncle had stopped short of disowning Jarrod when he learned his son was gay, but he'd asked Jarrod to leave Tulsa, fearing his son's lifestyle would negatively impact Dawson Investments' reputation.

A reputation that was at risk if Wade didn't recover Samantha's trust fund.

"So…" She waved a hand in the air. "What was the reason again you couldn't climb a tree?"

"Guess I got sidetracked." He grinned. "There weren't any opportunities to climb trees at the boys' private school. I did take a fencing class but my glasses slipped too often and I usually ended up on the losing side of a saber."

"What about horseback riding?"

"Tried that, too, but couldn't stay in the saddle." The horse had bolted as soon as he'd put his foot in the stirrup. Wade had clung to the saddle horn for almost a mile, one foot dragging against the ground. When the animal finally slowed and he'd been able to free his foot, he'd twisted his ankle and had ended up on crutches for a month. From that day forward, Wade stuck to studying during his free time. "I don't remember my uncle ever mentioning where you went to college."

The fork hesitated midway to her mouth, then she shoveled the food inside, chewed and swallowed. As if she hadn't heard his previous statement, she said, "I'm debating whether or not to build a storage barn in addition to a large horse barn on the property."

Dollar signs flew around in Wade's head. "How many barns do you need?"

"A smaller structure would be nice to store extra feed and farm equipment."

"You mean tractors?"

"Plows and harvest machines. I intend to use half the land to plant hay and alfalfa."

Farm equipment would cost hundreds of thousands of dollars. "Why go to all the trouble to grow crops when you can buy the feed?" Samantha's sanctuary ranch was turning into a huge financial commitment that would require her to hire hands to manage.

"Rescued horses need more than hay and grain. They need to graze grass to put on weight." Her expression softened. "I want the horses that come to my ranch to have the very best."

The conviction in her voice proved that Wade's initial impression of Samantha had been off the mark. This wasn't a pet project she'd tire of after a while. She genuinely cared about rehabilitating horses and providing a safe environment for the animals to recover from the neglect they'd suffered. "You're a special woman." His heart thumped hard inside his chest when her gaze dropped to his mouth.

Did she want to kiss him as much as he wanted to kiss her?

He inched forward, tilting his head. Then paused when her breath puffed against his face. He waited for a signal that he should proceed. When her dark lashes fluttered closed, he brushed his lips across hers. Gentle…slow… He tested the waters. Her mouth tasted of tangy barbecue and a heady…dark…erotic flavor. He pressed his lips harder against hers.

"Ouch!"

He jerked upright. "What happened?"

"Your glasses." She rubbed her cheekbone below her left eye.

He brushed the pad of his thumb across the red mark marring her flawless skin. "Sorry."

She removed his glasses. "That's better."

Says who? Samantha's image blurred before his eyes.

Clasping his face between her hands, she whispered, "I'll guide you." Her lips drew a rumbling groan from his chest as she slid her tongue inside his mouth. Then Samantha shifted toward him and her plate tipped over on his lap.

"Oh!" She jumped off the swing and attempted to remove the pile of baked beans soaking the front of his jeans. Her fingers caused more damage than the spilled food and he brushed her hands away, hoping she hadn't felt his arousal when she'd pressed the napkin to his crotch.

"I'm so sorry, Wade." Her face glowed fire-hydrant red.

"That's okay." He brushed the beans onto his plate. "Where are my glasses?" She handed them over. "Thanks." Now that he could see better…jeez. "Looks like I messed my pants."

Samantha hooted. Not a laugh. Not a giggle. A *hoot*.

Wade smiled, pleased he'd tickled her funny bone. He glanced at his watch. *I want to stay.* "I'd better go." *I want to kiss you again.* "I've got business briefs to work on at home."

"Really?" She sounded disappointed.

He brushed a strand of loose hair behind her ear,

allowing his fingers to linger against her skin a moment before he forced himself to turn away and descend the porch steps. When he reached the car he waved. "See you tomorrow."

The drive to his condo was the longest of Wade's life. What had he been thinking—kissing Samantha? She was his client—reason enough to keep his hands off her. Never mind the fact that he hadn't been truthful about her missing money. If he knew what was good for him he'd steer clear of the cowgirl.

Chapter Eight

Wade was avoiding Samantha.

When she'd arrived at the Peterson homestead earlier in the morning, he'd been helping the cowboys dig a trench that would carry a water pipe from the new well to the paddocks. She'd stopped at his side to say "Good morning" and Wade had uttered a brief "Hi" before moving farther down the line to dig—not the greeting she'd expected after the kiss they'd shared yesterday.

Miffed, Sam had spent the remainder of the morning sulking and contemplating their porch kiss—the one that obviously hadn't made much of an impact on Wade. He had kissed the boots off her feet—not the kind of smooch she'd expected from Mr. Financial Adviser. Sam believed that buried deep beneath his Wall Street facade Wade yearned to cut loose and score. So why the cold shoulder? Maybe she'd read too much into a kiss she'd been aching for since they'd first met.

What did the kiss mean to you, Sam?

Nothing, her conscience protested.

Everything, her heart confessed.

When was the last time she'd felt the press of a man's mouth against hers? Two years ago with Bo.

She'd lived on a ranch all her life surrounded by ranch hands and rodeo cowboys. She adored strong, brooding men. Then she'd discovered not all cowboys walked the walk or talked the talk. Bo had taught her that she was only lovable when she didn't forget or mess up.

Wade's different.

Of course, he wasn't a cowboy. The more she hung around him the less she worried about her memory lapses. Wade was special—no one would convince her otherwise.

Yesterday when Matt's friends had poked fun at his skills with a shovel, Wade had laughed at himself right along with the others. Undeterred by the ribbing, he'd done more than his fair share of grunt work, earning the men's respect. From the beginning, Sam had believed digging a well by hand was a waste of time, but she found Wade's willingness to risk ridicule in order to save her money sweet and endearing.

"Hi, Miss Samantha." Luke had awoken from his nap beneath the hackberry tree and stood rubbing his sleep-swollen eyes. Her heart melted at the vulnerable picture he made—hair smashed down on one side of his head, shirt wrinkled and shoes untied. The boy looked anything but a genius.

"Mornin', buster." Then she added. "Why don't you call me Miss Sam. It's shorter."

"Dad says I have to be polite."

She resisted the urge to push his slipping glasses up the bridge of his nose. "Miss Sam is polite."

"If you say so." He shielded his eyes from the sun's glare. "Where's my dad?"

"Over there." She pointed to the paddocks where the men were taking a break.

"I promised Dad I'd help."

"You are helping," Sam insisted.

"I am?"

"You're keeping Millicent company."

"But I was sleeping."

"Watching you sleep makes her feel useful." When he scrunched his nose, she added, "Millicent doesn't have any family so she gets lonely."

"What happened to her family?"

"Her husband died in World War II and her son left home years ago. She never remarried, so she's been alone for a long time."

Luke scuffed the toe of his shoe in the dirt. "My mom says Dad's never gonna marry again."

Oh, really? "Why does she say that?" As soon as Sam asked, she wished she hadn't. Yes, she was nosy but she doubted Wade would appreciate his son sharing personal information.

"Mom says Dad's a dunce." Luke squinted at Sam. "I don't get it because my dad's really smart."

Sam suspected the chemistry had waned between the couple because Sam found nothing duncey about Wade or his kisses. "Your father is brilliant and you know what?"

"What?"

"He told me you were smarter than him. He's proud of you."

Luke's shoulders straightened. "School's easy."

Sam wished she felt the same way about learning.

"I remember all the stuff I read. Do you?"

"My memory isn't that good, but I make lots of notes so I won't forget."

"If you want, you can tell me stuff and I'll remember for you."

Tears burned Sam's eyes as she hugged the boy. "That's nice, Luke. Thank you."

"Go ahead. I'm ready," he said.

"Ready for what?"

"To remember stuff for you."

Sam pressed her lips together to keep from smiling at the boy's earnest expression. After a minute she said the first thing that popped into her mind. "I need to call the local veterinarian and ask him to stop by the ranch."

"Why?"

"He'll tell me what supplies to stock the barn with for the rescued horses."

"You're gonna rescue horses?"

"Yep."

"What are you rescuing them from?"

Bad people. "Unfortunate circumstances."

"Huh?"

Even though Luke was smarter than most adults, he was a kid and hopefully ignorant of the sad fact that innocent animals occasionally suffered neglect at their owner's hands. "When people lose their jobs or become ill and can no longer properly take care of their horses, the animals often starve or their injuries go untreated."

"What happens to the horses?"

"The SPCA rescues the animals, then after nursing them back to health they find people willing to adopt the horses or board them until permanent homes are found."

"You're gonna board them?"

"Yep."

"Can I help take care of the horses?"

"You and your dad live a long way from here. Plus you're busy with school."

"We could come on the weekends. And once you build a new house, Dad and I can stay overnight."

That sounded too much like being a family—and family was out of the question for Sam. "We'll see. Right now I..." The rest of her sentence trailed off when she spotted her father's Chevy Apache pickup parked next to the other ranch trucks.

Panic swelled inside her. She couldn't recall the date her father had intended to return from his business trip—as if that mattered now. "Would you mind checking on Millicent?"

When Luke didn't obey, Sam insisted, "Go on. I'll only be a few minutes."

"He looks mean," Luke whispered when Sam's father got out of the truck.

Not mean...determined. "It's the mustache." Sam flashed a reassuring smile and Luke shuffled off.

The cowboys waved to her father as he called several by name. Wade had stopped digging in the trench and stared. "Welcome home, Daddy." Sam met him at the truck.

"Don't you 'Daddy' me, young lady. What's going on here?"

Squaring her shoulders she said, "Matt's friends are laying a water pipe from the new well they dug to the paddocks." She pointed to white fence posts that had been cemented into the ground.

"Stop stalling, Samantha."

Here goes nothing. "Welcome to the Last Chance Ranch, Daddy."

After a strained pause, he said, "Start from the beginning."

Sam refused to have this conversation in public. "I don't have time to talk. We'll discuss this over supper."

Her father opened his mouth, then snapped it shut.

Whew! She'd won the first round. "Tell Juanita to expect me around six o'clock."

"You'd better not be a minute late, daughter."

"I'll be on time. Promise." As soon as her father climbed into his truck and drove off, Sam sighed in relief. She wasn't looking forward to the grilling she'd receive later, but at least she had a few hours to build up her defenses. She had to convince her father that she was ready for this challenge or he'd find an excuse to rein her in, as was his habit when she strayed too far.

"Trouble?"

Sam jumped at the sound of Wade's voice. "Maybe."

"I guess your father wasn't pleased you bought the Peterson homestead."

"Nope." Her gaze slid to his mouth.

"Anything I can do to help?"

Kiss me. "As a matter of fact there is."

"What's that?"

"Daddy invited you and Luke to join us for dinner tonight." Sam walked off, leaving Wade with his luscious mouth hanging open.

DAMN. WHAT ROTTEN LUCK.

Wade had planned to review the building's security tape this coming Monday and ID the man who'd snuck into Dawson Investments on July fourth. He'd hoped the intruder's identity would lead Wade to Samantha's trust fund. Then he'd intended to schedule a meeting to apprise Samantha and Dominick of the situation. Now those plans had been threatened by an unexpected dinner invitation that would no doubt turn into an inquisition.

Samantha had left an hour ago with orders not to procrastinate. Wade had insisted on staying until the cowboys had cleaned up the day's projects when in truth he'd needed time to prepare for meeting the oil baron.

"All done, Dad," Luke said, shaking his freshly washed hands.

Wade glanced at his watch. They'd delayed long enough. As it was he'd have to push the speed limit to arrive at the Lazy River on time. "Let's go."

"Wait." Luke tugged Wade's shirtsleeve, then pointed to the water witch rocking beneath the tree. "Isn't Millicent coming?"

"I don't think so."

"Hey, Millicent," Luke shouted. "You wanna come eat with us at Miss Sam's?"

The old woman slapped at the air with her hand. "Got me vittles right here. Go on with ya."

Once the BMW turned onto the county road, Luke said, "Millicent lied."

"What do you mean?"

"She doesn't have much food in her house. Miss

Sam brings her fruit and stuff but mostly she eats biscuits."

"Old people don't need a lot of food."

"Dad?"

"What?"

"Millicent needs a family."

His son had a soft heart—even after all the teasing he'd suffered before he'd transferred to the boys' school. "Miss Samantha will be her family when she builds a new house at the ranch."

"Millicent said Miss Sam—"

"It's Miss Samantha."

"She said I could call her Miss Sam." Luke rolled his eyes. "Millicent said Miss Sam has lots of angels looking out for her."

"Why's that?"

Luke shrugged.

Wade tucked the tidbit of information away for middle-of-the-night insomnia, which he'd suffered from since meeting Samantha. Father and son drove the rest of the way in silence. As soon as the car passed beneath the tall black arches Luke asked, "Is this it?"

"Welcome to the Lazy River."

"Where's the river?" Luke pressed his face against the window.

"There is none." Wade's uncle had explained that at one time a river had flowed through the property but after the great Dust Bowl of the 1930s, the water had dried to a trickle. Wade suspected the name had to do with the river being too lazy to flow.

Wade parked in front of the main house, his eyes zeroing in on the porch swing. He forced the memory of his and Samantha's kiss to the back of his mind—he couldn't afford any distractions tonight.

The housekeeper met them at the door. "Luke, this is Señora Juanita."

"Hello, Luke." Juanita opened the door. "Come. Sam and Señor Cartwright wait for you." She ushered them into the dining room.

Wade paused in the doorway, placing his hand on Luke's shoulder. His gaze sought out Samantha first.

"Welcome, Wade." Her smile loosened the knot in his stomach. "Sit here, Luke." She patted the seat next to her.

Wade's forehead broke out in a sweat when Dominick stood at the head of the table. He moved forward and shook hands with the older man. "Wade Dawson. Pleasure meeting you again, sir."

"Charlie's nephew, right?"

"Yes, sir." Wade sat across from Samantha. Before he introduced his son, Juanita entered the room and set a plate of fried chicken in the center of the table, then added a bowl of potato salad and fresh fruit. "Enjoy."

"Luke, this is Mr. Cartwright, Miss Samantha's father. Mr. Cartwright, I'd like you to meet my son, Luke."

"Did you know that the year your truck was made the population of the United States was over a hundred and seventy-seven million. And life expectancy was almost seventy years old?" Luke directed the question to Dominick.

Wade swallowed a groan. When the boy became nervous he spouted off trivia.. Luke must want to make a good impression on Samantha's father.

"You don't say." Dominick's eyebrow rose in amusement. "Anything interesting happen in 1979?"

"Kylene Baker won the Miss America pageant. She was from Virginia."

"Quite a bright mind you've got there, young man."

"Yeah, I'm really smart. Dad says I'm a genius." Luke helped himself to a chicken leg. "But I only memorize stuff when I get really bored."

"How often are you bored?" Dominick asked.

"Not a lot because at my school all the kids are smart like me."

"Glad to hear you're keeping the teachers on their toes." Dominick shifted his attention to Wade. "I wasn't aware you'd married?"

Not surprising. Uncle Charles rarely spoke about Wade to his clients or friends. "I've been divorced for three years."

"Why didn't you talk my daughter out of purchasing the Peterson property?" Dominick's gaze swung between Wade and Samantha.

Wade expected Samantha to head off the question but she remained silent and played with the potato salad on her plate. "The property had been purchased before she came to me to access her trust fund."

Dominick tossed a glare his daughter's way but she'd struck up a conversation with Luke, leaving Wade to bear the brunt of her father's disapproval. "Samantha's intent to open a horse sanctuary is a worthy cause," Wade lied through his teeth. He didn't understand his need to defend her, but he suspected it had to do with the kiss they'd shared yesterday.

That damned kiss had clung to his conscience like a

bad investment. He liked Samantha. A lot. Maybe more than a lot. But he had no right to allow their relationship to move in a personal direction until he told her the truth about the missing money.

Then tell her and be done with it.

Wade prided himself on being an honest, ethical investor but if he came clean before he located Samantha's trust fund she'd view him as a screwup when in fact he'd earned the firm's title of top investor three years running. Wade didn't possess any impressive cowboy qualities—he couldn't ride a horse or bust a bull or even dig a damned well. If he intended to pursue a relationship with Samantha all he had to wow her with was his financial acumen.

"There's nothing fiscally sound about rescuing horses." Dominick interrupted Wade's thoughts.

"Samantha will gain a substantial tax write-off. And once the initial costs of renovating the property are met, she can then apply for federal grants to subsidize her operation," Wade argued.

Dominick narrowed his eyes. *Oh, hell.* The man knew Wade was spouting bullshit off the top of his head. "And," Wade continued, "Samantha's generosity and good works won't go unnoticed. The sanctuary will be fantastic PR for Cartwright Oil." Wade's pinched lungs relaxed when Dominick offered a grudging nod.

"Miss Sam's gonna teach me how to ride a horse," Luke said. "Right, Miss Sam?"

Samantha's eyes clashed with her father's and Wade was shocked when Dominick's expression turned stormy.

Oblivious to the tension at the table Luke rambled. "Miss Sam has to teach me because my dad's not good at stuff like riding horses and climbing trees. But that's okay because he's really smart like me. Aren't you, Dad?"

Embarrassed, Wade said, "Finish your dinner, Luke." Everyone took Wade's words to heart and ate in silence until they'd cleaned their plates.

When Juanita announced chocolate cake for dessert, Dominick rose from his chair. "Wade and I will have dessert in my office. We have business to discuss." Then he suggested to Samantha, "Why don't you show Luke my truck?"

"Awesome!" Luke jumped off his chair.

Wade noticed that Samantha didn't appreciate her father's suggestion. As soon as Dominick left the room, she whispered, "Make him understand, Wade."

How was he supposed to make Dominick understand the importance of Samantha's project when Wade didn't even know why it meant so much to her? But one look in her pretty brown eyes and he was lost. "I'll try." He'd do more than try, because his own ass was in the line of fire.

Dominick's office reeked of wealth. Imported leather chairs, a mahogany desk and matching bookcases. Flat-screen TV on the wall and a minibar in the corner. A partially opened door revealed a private bathroom. The oil king motioned for Wade to sit.

"Why wasn't I informed about my daughter's visit to Dawson Investments?" The man didn't mince words.

Wade wished Samantha would give up her rescue ranch so he'd be temporarily spared from exposing Dawson Investments' negligence but at the same time he wanted her to succeed, even at the risk of losing his pro-motion at the firm. "Samantha came to our office on her thirty-second birthday—legally entitled to access any amount of money from her trust without your signature."

"I should have had that changed but I set up the account before the accident and never—" He stopped speaking abruptly and stared into space.

"Sir?"

"What's done is done," Dominick said. "Tell me how you propose to manage her withdrawals."

"There isn't much to manage." God's honest truth.

"You're dolling out my hard-earned money blindly? What kind of a financial adviser are you?"

Swallowing a curse, Wade explained. "When Samantha asked for large sums of cash to make several improvements to the Peterson property, I convinced her to focus on one project at a time, so that the remainder of her funds would continue to collect interest."

"I'm relieved to hear that. Ever since the accident, I've worried she'll be taken advantage of."

What accident?

"Sir, this project means a lot to your daughter. I'll make sure she spends her money responsibly. In the end if the horse sanctuary doesn't work out the property will be ready for a quick sale."

"You make a valid point. For now I'll trust you to keep a close eye on her."

If Dominick only knew what a dangerous proposition that was.

"When you have time I'd like you to send me a record of her withdrawals and where the money's gone." It was an order not a request.

"Absolutely." After viewing the security tape Wade would be able to come clean with Samantha and her father.

"It's good my daughter has you to look after her. Now that Matt and Duke have moved away she needs another big brother."

Ouch. Wade's ego winced. No man appreciated being categorized as a harmless pup. "I'm managing her portfolio, sir, not her life."

The oil baron ignored Wade's comment and shuffled through a stack of papers on his desk, in effect dismissing Wade.

"Is there anything else, sir?"

"No. I'm leaving my daughter's affairs in your capable hands."

If Dominick had witnessed the way Wade had kissed Samantha yesterday he wouldn't be leaving his daughter anywhere near Wade.

Chapter Nine

After three cups of Juanita's kick-ass coffee, Sam drove away from the Lazy River filled with self-doubts and uncertainty about using her new ranch as a horse sanctuary—thanks to her recent nightmare.

Last night she'd suffered a setback. Matt had always woken her before the nightmare escalated, but this time her protector hadn't been there and Sam had screamed out loud. Her father had practically kicked in the bedroom door to get to her. Even after repeated attempts to reassure him she was fine, his face had remained pale and his hands had trembled as he'd rubbed her back.

When he'd left her alone an hour later, Sam had sat on the edge of her bed and cried silent tears. Her accident years ago had not only changed her life forever but had affected the lives of everyone in her family, especially her father.

For years she'd suffered nightmares, but she'd never considered that her father might be experiencing the same misery down the hall in his bedroom. Now she carried the burden of his fear along with her own as she embarked on this journey to put the past behind her.

Was she doing the right thing or not? Would tackling her fears alleviate her father's misgivings and concerns or increase them? Until the nightmare Sam hadn't acknowledged that she'd gone into this undertaking halfheartedly. If she stuck with her plans to open a sanctuary ranch, then she had to throw herself behind the project one hundred percent. Even if no one else believed in her—she had to believe in herself if she intended to succeed.

After her accident her father hadn't left her hospital bedside, sleeping and showering in her private room until she'd awoken from her coma. During the long months of therapy that followed he'd been her loudest cheerleader. Each time she'd threatened to give up—and there had been many—he'd refused to allow her to quit.

Doubts assailed Sam. She could give this ranch her all but that didn't guarantee she had the skills or knowledge to deal with unexpected situations. Even though she intended to board the more docile horses from the SPCA how would she react if one of the horses went loco? Would she panic or remain calm enough to keep herself and the horse safe? Failing wasn't an option. She refused to put herself and her father through all this stress only to give up in the end.

She spotted the entrance to the Oklahoma SPCA equine center and shoved her worries to the back of her mind. After parking the truck next to the horse barn, she headed across the dirt lot, calling to the three mares grazing in a paddock.

Nancy Parker stepped out of the office and waved. "Morning, Samantha." Nancy was the head honcho for the equine center and had managed the facility for over fifteen years. Sam had shared her plans to open a sanctuary ranch with the manager months ago. Nancy had been the one to suggest that Sam work with horses under her supervision before she purchased the Peterson homestead.

"How's the ranch coming along?" Nancy led the way into the horse barn.

"The paddocks are up. The well is dug. I'm waiting on a barn now."

"Great. I'd love for you to take Blue when you're ready." She stopped outside the gelding's stall.

Sam had worked with the horse several times and the animal had never made a threatening move toward Sam. "He's such a gentle guy. Why hasn't the SPCA found him a home yet?"

"Too many scars. People want a pretty horse."

Blue had gotten tangled in a barbed wire fence and had fought so viciously to escape he'd almost killed himself. One ear had been severed and there were multiple scars crisscrossing his body as well as a huge chunk of muscle on his chest that had become infected and had to be cut away.

"What you're doing is really special, Samantha." Nancy handed Sam a carrot to feed the horse. "I didn't expect to find a foster home for Blue when he first arrived. I thought he'd be with us forever. Now he'll be able to live out the rest of his years in comfort."

"Besides Blue, will the other horses I foster have a chance to be adopted?"

"We'll continue to evaluate each horse's progress after they settle in at your ranch, then we'll screen potential owners and bring them out to meet the animals. Maybe we'll get lucky."

"What if I make a mistake handling the horses?" Sam hated that she sounded insecure.

Nancy moved to the next stall where a pregnant mare munched on hay. "Having second thoughts?"

"Maybe," Sam admitted.

After a solemn stare, Nancy said, "Did you know that your father used to be one of our biggest supporters?"

"What do you mean, used to?"

"After your accident, he stopped making donations to the SPCA."

That didn't surprise Sam. The horse that kicked her in the head had been adopted from the SPCA. Sam's father felt responsible for her accident since he'd given the horse to her for her sixteenth birthday. "I'm sorry, I didn't—"

"Is Dominick aware you're working with SPCA horses?"

"Yes." Sam rushed on. "But he doesn't like it."

"If my child had almost lost her life because of a horse, I'd want them to stay as far away from the animals as possible." Nancy stopped at the last stall in the barn and clicked her tongue. Red lifted his head from the feed bucket, snorted, then ignored them.

"You have the financial means to foster horses and to renovate the Peterson property, but you have to be one hundred percent comfortable working with these animals. It would be irresponsible of me to hand over a horse if you're not ready. I would never forgive myself if you were injured."

"I'm still nervous around horses, but I miss the special bond I had with these animals." She sucked in a quiet breath. "Like Blue, I have to face my fears and learn to trust again." *Until I do, I'm no good to anyone.*

Nancy flashed a sympathetic smile. "You've made great strides since coming here. If you want, I'll teach you a few tricks to help you relax around the horses. But I want your promise that if any of the horses give you trouble you'll tell me."

The knot in Sam's stomach loosened. "Promise."

"Great. I left a list of exercises I'd like Blue to do this morning. Why don't you work with him on those."

"Sure." Sam spent the next two hours saddling and unsaddling Blue. The horse never protested and she rewarded his patience with a carrot. After returning the saddle to the tack room Sam drove out to the Peterson property. She'd hired a local company to regrade the road leading to the farmhouse. Once a fresh layer of gravel was put down a construction crew would begin assembling the new horse barn. Thinking she'd better inform Wade about the roadwork scheduled for today, she dialed his cell number. He answered on the second ring.

"Wade Dawson."

The sound of his deep voice teased a sigh from her heart. "Hi, Wade. It's me, Sam."

"Samantha, how are you?"

"Why don't you call me Sam?"

"I like Samantha. It's sophisticated and elegant."

Talk about absurd—she was the farthest thing from sophistication and elegance.

"How can I help you?" he asked.

What was up with the Mr. Manners routine? "I figured you'd want to know that I hired a crew to regrade the road on the Peterson property."

Was that a groan she heard on the other end of the line?

"Give me the name and phone number of the company. I'll make sure they send the bill to my office."

Sam read off the number in her notebook. After an awkward silence she said, "That's all I wanted to tell you. Have a good day."

"Sam, wait!"

She smiled. "You called me Sam."

"Sorry. Slipup. Are you free for lunch?"

"Today?" She held her breath.

"I'd planned on paying off your account at Barney's Ranch Supply in person." He expelled a loud breath. "Since I'm driving all the way out there I wondered if you'd have lunch with me."

Like a teenager with her first crush, Sam's pulse raced.

"A business lunch," he continued.

Not a date? Her enthusiasm waned.

"We need to discuss the next item on your ranch-improvement list after the road is fixed."

Great. "Let's meet at Beulah's. It's a few miles south of Barney's."

"How does one o'clock sound?" he asked.

"Fine. See you then." She hung up before he changed his mind.

If Sam got lucky maybe their business lunch would end on a more personal note—a kiss.

"Excuse me, Mr. Dawson. The security tape arrived." Veronica stood in the hall outside Wade's office. How long had she eavesdropped on his conversation with Samantha? He motioned for her to come in and she slid a CD onto his desk.

"Thank you." The security company had promised

the footage this past Monday. Two days late, Wade was eager to view the CD. He walked Veronica to the door. "If my uncle checks in with you this morning transfer him to my line."

"Yes, sir."

Wade closed his office door, then inserted the CD into his computer drive. Not more than five minutes of viewing had passed before Wade's mind wandered to Samantha. *Sam.* The nickname just didn't seem to do her justice.

He hadn't intended to pay the bill at the ranch supply store in person—it was a waste of gas and time. If Sam hadn't phoned him he'd have sent Barney a check in the mail. Hearing her voice moments ago reminded him how much he'd missed her this week. It didn't matter how many times he told himself that becoming involved with Samantha on a personal level was a bad idea until he recovered her trust fund. Where Sam was concerned, Wade had no willpower.

What the heck? Wade paused the CD, then rewound the footage and pressed Play. A man wearing khaki pants and a dark red golf shirt strolled through the lobby to the elevator bank. He stepped into the elevator and turned. As if Wade had been sucker punched, the air burst from his lungs.

Uncle Charles. Had the old man used a phony ID to withdraw funds from Samantha's account?

His uncle exited the elevator at Dawson Investments, then waltzed through the doors before the screen went black. Three seconds later the security camera inside the office began recording. His uncle strolled down the hallway and entered Wade's office.

I'll be damned.

Five agonizing minutes of a blank screen—there were no security cameras in the individual offices—before his uncle returned to his own office. A few minutes later, Charles left the building.

His uncle must have accessed the security codes for Samantha's account from Wade's files. Wade dialed his uncle's cell phone and got his voice mail—par for the course. He left a message to call back ASAP. An hour passed and he hadn't heard from his uncle. Fuming, Wade paced in front of his desk.

All he'd ever wanted was to please his uncle. And how had the man chosen to repay Wade's loyalty—by using him as a pawn in whatever financial scheme his uncle had become involved in. Wade prayed it wasn't too late to recover Samantha's money.

Agitated, he grabbed his suit coat and left the office. At least he had lunch with Samantha to look forward to—the one bright spot in an otherwise miserable day.

THE BELL ABOVE THE DOOR to Barney's Ranch Supply clanged when Wade entered the building. He paused to allow his eyes to adjust to the dim interior. Dust particles danced in the stream of sunlight that entered the store with him. The place smelled of wood rot, old leather and manure.

"Ya gonna shut the door or invite all the flies in?" a craggy voice asked.

Wade closed the door, then maneuvered around tables of merchandise and clothing racks circa 1980s apparel. The warped floorboards popped beneath his shoes and mold spores tickled his nose.

"You must be Barney," Wade said, stopping next to

the checkout counter where an old man slouched in a chair. An open bag of potato chips sat on the counter, its contents spilling across a pile of invoices, dotting the papers with grease stains. A fifth of Jim Beam and a can of Diet Coke sat next to the chips.

Barney stood, then snapped his suspenders against his potbelly. "Watcha want with me?"

"I'm Wade Dawson, Samantha Cartwright's financial adviser." He offered a hand and Barney offered greasy fingers.

"Come to pay that gal's bill?" The store's proprietor brushed at the crumbs sticking to the front of his white cotton T-shirt.

Wade turned his head and sneezed. "Excuse me."

"For what?" Barney grumbled, shuffling through the invoices on the counter.

"For sneezing." Wade's nose twitched again, but he pinched his nostrils together to halt the sneeze.

"What's a matter? Do I stink?" Barney held out an invoice.

"Allergies." Wade squinted at the chicken scratch on the piece of paper. He didn't see a dollar amount. "What are the total charges?"

"Well, now, that depends."

Right then a black cat jumped off a shelf above Barney's head and landed on top of the potato chip bag, scaring the crap out of Wade. The feline stretched out across the invoices, its tail swishing back and forth, knocking pieces of broken chips to the floor.

"Depends on what?" Wade asked.

"On whether Sam meant to double her order of tools fer that new barn she's puttin' up at the Peterson place."

"What do you mean, double her order?"

Barney rubbed his whiskered cheeks. "Sam called Monday 'n again yesterday orderin' the same supplies. I reckon she's confused."

Confused—what did that mean? "Hold off on the second order. I'll check with Samantha when we meet for lunch today."

"Then ya owe me $6,012.15."

Wade handed him a certified check for seven thousand dollars.

"Ain't got but twenty dollars in the change drawer."

"Credit Samantha's account with the rest." From now on Wade intended to call in Samantha's orders and deal directly with Barney.

"I reckon ya'll be wantin' a receipt. Ya city folk's gotta have everythin' on paper." Barney scribbled a note on the back of an old invoice, then shuffled through the mess on the counter until he uncovered a rubber stamp and ink pad. He pounded the stamp against the pad, then banged it on the paper. *PAID* stood out in bright red letters. "There's yer receipt."

"Thank you." Wade slipped the note into his pocket.

"We done now?"

"I need directions to Beulah's."

"Got a hankerin' fer pig's feet, have ya?" At Wade's frown, Barney added, "Beulah runs a special on Wednesdays—pickled pig's feet."

Wade would not be sampling the *special* today. He set his business card beneath the cat's swishing tail. "Call me if Samantha places another order and I'll give you a credit card number over the phone."

"Don't take credit cards."

Since when did a business not accept a credit card as payment?

"You can leave a check with Sam or Millicent. They'll get me the money."

"Millicent doesn't drive." The dowsing queen couldn't see more than five feet in front of her.

"Sure she does. Takes that old Bel-Air in the barn fer a spin every once 'n while."

Wade suspected the last time the old woman had driven, Nixon had been president. "I'll bring the check by."

"Suit yerself." Barney clicked his false teeth and the cat's ears perked.

Wade sneezed again. He had to get out of there before his eyes swelled shut. "Where did you say Beulah's was?"

"Didn't yet. Ya hijacked the conversation."

Swallowing his impatience, Wade said, "I apologize."

"Ain't nothin' to apologize fer. Some folks jest got the need to yak is all."

"Barney, where is Beulah's?"

"Go out to the main road 'n take a left. Her place is 'bout a mile down on the right. Pink house. Can't miss it."

"Thanks." As soon as Wade left the store he sucked in several deep breaths, clearing the mold spores and cat hairs from his nostrils. He followed Barney's directions and spotted Beulah's—a bubble-gum pink Victorian sitting in the middle of nowhere.

Glossy black shutters and a black front door decorated the home. The upper-story windows were open and lace curtains blew in the breeze. A black iron fence surrounded the property and in the middle of the yard stood a sign as big as a billboard with *Beulah's* written in fancy black script against a pink background. The place reminded Wade of a nineteenth-century bordello complete with chickens pecking the dirt driveway.

He parked in the lot behind the house, noting two sheriff's vehicles among the slew of pickups—an indication Beulah served a decent lunch. When he spotted Samantha's truck his blood pumped a little faster. In the back, there was a patio crowded with black resin tables shaded by pink umbrellas. The place was packed with men—ranch hands, deputies and cowboys. Samantha sat in the middle of the sea of testosterone, her long hair glinting in the sunlight. The patrons at the table had their eyes glued to her beautiful face.

Jealousy zapped Wade square in the gut, but he resisted the urge to morph into a caveman, throw Samantha over his shoulder and race off with her. One kiss didn't mean he had any claim on her.

But you wish it did.

The chance of entering a lasting relationship with Samantha would be zero-to-none after he revealed Dawson Investments had lost—make that stolen—her trust fund. Wade's first responsibility was to his client, then the firm. He preferred to confront his uncle before coming clean with Samantha, but decided to break the news to her over lunch today.

In a suit and tie he'd stand out like a sore thumb among the cowboys, so Wade shrugged out of his jacket and tossed his tie across the front seat. Then he rolled up his sleeves. He couldn't do anything about his glasses except push them up the bridge of his nose. The patio gate emitted a loud squeak when he opened it.

Samantha flashed a beautiful smile, then met him on

the sidewalk. He was aware of the envious stares he attracted and decided he liked being the guy with the beautiful woman for a change.

"Hi," she said. "Hungry?"

"Starved." *For you.* Her smile widened and his chest tightened. Samantha was good for his ego—he didn't have to do or be anything extraordinary to measure up in her eyes. A sharp stab of conscience reminded him that her feelings would change after she learned the truth about her financial situation.

"Beulah's got a table for us inside." She took his hand and led him into the house through a back door, then down a narrow hallway to a parlor at the front of the house. Samantha stopped at the table next to a window with a view of a garden. As soon as they were seated a large woman waddled into the room delivering water glasses and menus.

"This the man ya been waitin' fer?" Dressed from head to toe in a pink muumuu and wearing black ballet slippers, the woman scrutinized Wade.

"Beulah, this is Wade Dawson. Wade this is Beulah."

"Nice to meet you, Beulah."

"Likewise. Today's special is pickled pig's feet."

Samantha didn't bother perusing the menu. "I'll have the club sandwich and fruit salad."

Wade didn't want to waste their time together. "The same for me."

"Too bad. My pig's feet is juicy and tender." She snatched the menus off the table and disappeared.

"Did you have trouble finding Beulah's?" Sam swallowed a groan at the stupid question. Why so nervous all of a sudden? Lunch had been Wade's suggestion not hers.

His gaze dropped to her mouth and her stomach flipped upside down. "This is the only pink house for miles."

Flustered, she asked, "Did you stop by Barney's?"

"I paid the bill and you have a nine-hundred-dollar credit on your account." He sipped his water, then added, "Barney said you'd confused him with the last order you called in."

"Oh?" Panic raced through her. She couldn't remember her previous conversation with the store owner.

"You ordered tools and supplies for the new barn, then called the next day and placed a second order for the same items. He wondered if you were building two barns on the property."

Oh, God. She was busted. *Calm down. Take a deep breath. Relax.*

"You aren't considering two barns, are you?"

"Not right away," she answered, flushing. "I must have misspoke."

"Barney's an interesting character."

Grateful Wade didn't press her about the mix-up on the supply order, Sam relaxed. "I've known him since I was a little girl."

"Is he married?"

"No. He's been after Beulah to tie the knot with him for years, but she's sworn off men after her first love left her for a younger woman." Sam was dying to learn more about what happened between Wade and his ex-wife, but chickened out and asked about his son instead. "How's Luke?"

"He's eager to return to the ranch and help out this weekend."

"Saturday they begin construction of a new aluminum horse barn."

"*They* meaning your brother's cowboy buddies?"

"No. I hired a local construction company." Her answer elicited a frown from Wade. "What's wrong?"

"I wish you'd check with me before spending more money."

The whole money budgeting thing was getting on Sam's nerves. "Is it really necessary to keep close tabs on what I spend? The cost of renovating the ranch won't make a dent in my trust fund."

"The more withdrawals from your account the more penalties you'll incur." His hand clenched the fork next to his water glass until his knuckles whitened. "If I'm informed ahead of time what your plans are I'll withdraw enough money to cover several projects and you'll incur fewer penalties."

Or you'll try to talk me into holding off on the project. Not wishing to argue about the ranch, she said, "I'm sorry. I'll do better about keeping you informed." Not an easy task when she barely remembered her plans from one day to the next.

"Won't be long before the property is ready for horses. Are you excited?" he asked.

"Yes and no," she answered honestly.

"I'm listening." He flashed an encouraging smile.

The urge to confide in Wade tugged at Sam, but she hated exposing her shortcomings. She wanted Wade to view her as confident, assured and reasonable. "I'm eager to help the horses but I wish the renovations on the ranch were completed."

"I imagine fostering neglected horses will be a

change from caring for the spirited thoroughbreds you grew up with."

She let Wade's assumption pass without correcting him. "I'm worried that no matter how much I work with the animals I might not be able to help them." What she really wished to share with Wade was her fear that she'd panic if a horse became too spirited.

Wade rubbed his thumb across her knuckles, distracting her. "Don't underestimate yourself," he said. "You're a determined woman." Sam melted under his warm gaze. "Speaking from experience," he continued, "the rescued horses won't stand a chance against your sweetness."

Oh, Lord. Wade knew just what to say to make her heart skip a beat. His smile reeled her in and for a moment she imagined becoming intimately involved with him. Wade believed in her. Supported her choices. Encouraged her to pursue her heart's desire. It would be so easy to fall in love with him.

"I want this ranch to succeed. I've dreamed of becoming involved in a worthwhile project and now that it's within reach I'm concerned something will happen to jinx the dream."

Wade dropped his gaze to the tabletop and cleared his throat. "Samantha," he said, "there's something I've wanted to tell you for a while now."

His nervousness could only mean one thing—he was as attracted to her as she was to him. Her heart soared at the idea that they'd both been thinking along the same lines—wanting more than simple kisses from each other. "Me, too, Wade."

He glanced at her, his eyes wide with surprise. "What are you talking about?" he asked hesitantly.

"I feel the same way about you," she whispered, leaning across the narrow table until their mouths were only inches apart. "I really like you, Wade." She pressed her lips to his and shuddered when he groaned.

The kiss went on forever, his lips serenading hers with the sweetest touches, nibbles and flicks of his tongue. When he pulled back, desire swirled in his brown eyes and Sam knew she wanted all of Wade—preferably in her bed.

Chapter Ten

Thursday morning Samantha lounged by the pool after swimming laps. She'd needed the physical exercise to take the edge off the aroused state she'd woken in earlier—not that she'd minded her restless night in bed.

Her sleep had been filled with dreams of her and Wade making love. She blamed the erotic images on the kiss they'd shared at lunch yesterday. She'd never been so bold with a man, but Wade drew her to him in a way she didn't understand and had no control over. She preferred to believe her attraction to Wade was purely physical, but when she gazed into his dark brown eyes her heart convinced her otherwise.

Tired of fretting over her feelings for a man she could never be with, Sam donned her bathrobe and headed inside to confront a different obstacle—her father. She marched through the house to his office, then paused outside the door. "Got a minute, Daddy?"

He motioned to the chair in front of the desk. No smile. No greeting. Except when he'd comforted her after her nightmare, she'd been the recipient of the proverbial *cold shoulder* since her father had returned from his business trip and discovered that she'd purchased the Peterson property.

The time had come to clear the air between them. She claimed the leather chair in front of his desk, and fiddled with the tie on her robe in an attempt to conceal her frayed nerves. Out of respect for her father, she allowed him to speak first.

"I hear you've taken a leave of absence from your job." He tossed his reading glasses onto the desk.

The *job* he referenced was a glorified public relations position that required no other skills than being able to stuff Cartwright Oil brochures into envelopes and mail them. Her father had created the PR job because he felt sorry for her when she'd moped around the house after graduating from high school while her classmates prepared for college. College had been out of the question because of her memory difficulties. Sam believed her father had been relieved when she'd agreed to work in his offices—easier to keep an eye on her and ensure she came to no harm.

Whether her plans to open a sanctuary ranch succeeded or not, Sam refused to remain in a job that made her feel useless. "I won't be returning to work."

"Ever?"

In case her father intended to sabotage her new project, hoping its failure would force Sam to reconsider, she confirmed, "Not ever."

"Why didn't you discuss purchasing the Peterson property with me?"

She'd bruised her father's feelings when she hadn't sought his counsel before contacting a Realtor. "I had enough money saved to buy the ranch without dipping into my trust fund."

"Where did you get that kind of money?"

Was he serious? Her father paid her an outrageous salary. She had no social life. No significant other to spend money on. She lived at home. Had few bills. Her paychecks went straight into the bank. "I spent little of the salary you paid me."

An exasperated huff burst from him. "I deserved to know what my daughter intended to use her inheritance for." He waved a hand in the air. "If Matt hadn't leaked your secret when I spoke with him a week ago, I might never have learned your plans for this horse ranch you intend to operate."

Oh, dear. She should have expected her secret wouldn't remain sacred for long. "I didn't tell you, Daddy, because I knew you'd try to change my mind." Like he'd done each time she'd ventured too far from the safety net he'd cast over her after the accident.

"You're damned right I would have protested. This is a foolish, dangerous game you're playing with your life, Samantha. You can't expect me to stand aside and watch—" He swallowed hard and dropped his gaze to the desk calendar.

Sam hurt for her father. She couldn't remember the month following her accident, but her brothers had said their father refused to let her out of his sight during those thirty days. "I want you to keep me safe, Daddy."

"Then let me," he pleaded, his voice hoarse.

Sam launched herself out of the chair, skirted the desk and went down on her knees at her father's side.

"If I'm ever going to have the life I want, I need to prove I can stand on my own two feet."

"After your injuries, honey, no one expects you to—"

"*I* expect me to. I realize you only meant to protect me, but you should have let me go."

His face paled and Sam rushed to explain. "I should have ridden a horse as soon as the doctor gave the okay. Yes, I was frightened, but it was your fear, Daddy, that stopped me from trying." She wiped at a tear that escaped her eye. "I love horses. I want that part of my life back."

He cleared his throat. "I almost lost you, honey. It's not an experience a parent forgets. Ever."

"I'm a fighter, Daddy."

The corner of his mouth lifted. "You get that from me."

"Cartwrights don't walk away when the going gets tough," she said.

He shoved his fingers through his hair. "Why SPCA horses? They're unpredictable. Dangerous."

"For the past few months I've been caring for horses at the equine center. Just ones that are mild tempered and in need of a little TLC. I give you my word I won't go near the aggressive ones."

"If anything happens to you…" He clamped his mouth closed.

"Nancy Parker is teaching me how to rehabilitate abandoned and neglected horses." Sam squeezed his hand. "I'm positive I'll be ready to handle the animals once the ranch renovations are complete."

"Why didn't you tell me you'd been working at the SPCA?"

"Because you would have tried to stop me."

"Letting go is difficult," he admitted.

"You managed fine with Duke and then Matt."

"You'll come to me if you need anything? Anything at all?"

"Of course."

"And you won't object if I drop by the Peterson property to check up on you?"

"You're welcome anytime."

"Unannounced?" he added.

"What's that supposed to mean?"

"You and your financial adviser, Wade Dawson, appear to get along quite well."

Had her feelings for Wade been that transparent? Sam hopped up from the floor and moved to the window overlooking the front yard. "He frustrates me."

"Oh?"

"Wade won't loosen the reins on my money." She faced her father. "At the risk of sounding like a spoiled rich girl—"

"Which you are," her father inserted.

"—does it really matter if I pay top dollar for labor and construction materials when the cost of fixing up the property will barely make a dent in my funds?"

Her father grinned. "You could do worse than a man who possesses a healthy respect for money."

She worried her father hoped something might develop between her and Wade. Refusing to encourage him, she said, "Wade's too academic for me, Daddy. We don't have much in common."

"Don't sell yourself short, young lady. You have a lot to offer."

Maybe, but the one thing she couldn't offer was

being a mother to a man's child—even if that man was Wade and the child was Luke.

"Dawson's boy is quite a character."

"Luke's a sweet kid." And one she'd become far too attached to for her own good.

"Have you told Wade about your accident?"

"No." There wasn't any reason to unless she and Wade entered into a permanent relationship which would never happen.

"Is that wise?" Concern darkened her father's eyes.

Ignoring the heat rushing to her face, she insisted, "It isn't any of Wade's business." She changed the subject. "I'm driving out to Henderson Tractor-Trailer to buy a used trailer for the property."

"Temporary housing?" he asked.

She nodded. "I haven't decided whether to save or demolish the Peterson farmhouse."

When he opened his mouth to offer advice, Sam cut him off. "After I shop for trailers I'll be at the SPCA stables for a while."

Her father's smile didn't reach his eyes. "I'm a phone call away if you need me."

"Thanks, Daddy." After she got dressed, Sam left the house, feeling more positive than she had in a long while. The trailer shopping took less time than she'd anticipated thanks to Mr. Henderson's generosity. He'd agreed to deliver a showroom trailer to the Peterson property tomorrow morning. Next, she headed to the SPCA.

Although she was thrilled that her father had given her his support, she was well aware her plans to work with horses put him in a vulnerable position. If anything happened to her he'd never forgive himself for not intervening. She'd acted brave and self-assured in front of him—she could do no less. But deep down, Sam admitted that although she'd become more confident around horses, there were moments she experienced panic attacks.

When she arrived at the SPCA, she noticed that Blue, Red and Whisper were in the paddocks. Nancy's truck was nowhere in sight and the SPCA trailer was absent from its parking spot. Deciding to work with Blue on her own, she retrieved a grooming belt from the tack room in the horse barn. She adjusted the belt round her hips and checked to make sure she had all the proper grooming tools.

Blue had yet to allow her or anyone at the SPCA to groom him. The gelding's wounds had healed but Sam believed the pain from his injuries was still fresh in the horse's mind and when the brush touched the scars the animal panicked. She entered the paddock quietly, so as not to startle the animals.

Two weeks ago she'd begun a routine with Blue— wearing the grooming belt in his presence. Each time Blue had reared up or run off. Then a few days ago when Sam had entered the paddock Blue had stood his ground. She'd walked up to him and stroked his neck but had refrained from using any of the combs.

Today Blue's ears perked when she advanced toward him and he swished his tail in welcome. Sam rubbed his nose. "Hey, Blue. How's my favorite guy?"

He stomped his foot and, unprepared for the movement, Sam's heart jumped inside her chest. She moved to his side, then ran her fingers lightly over the worst of the scarring across his chest and left shoulder. His muscles tensed and Sam held her breath, forcing herself to keep her hand against the puckered flesh. After a few seconds, Blue relaxed and dipped his head into the grain bucket attached to the paddock post.

Slowly, Sam removed the soft-bristled body brush from the grooming belt. Normally she'd begin with the currycomb to loosen the dirt under the horse's hair but its rubber teeth would be too rough on Blue's sensitive scars. She allowed Blue to sniff the brush. The horse nudged the grooming tool, then gave a warning snort.

Sam wished she could give up and leave poor Blue alone, but if she walked away now Blue would win, and he'd never allow her or anyone to groom him. She had to show Blue that she was the boss and meant him no harm.

Deep breath. Sam slipped her hand beneath the strap across the back of the brush, then held it under Blue's nose again while she stroked his neck with her bare hand. Eventually Blue relaxed and Sam ran the bristles lightly across his hide, avoiding the scars. "See, Blue. You like this, don't you, big guy?"

After making sure she stood out of the way of Blue's hooves, Sam held her breath and placed the brush against the puckered flesh. Blue tensed. His belly filled with air. The whites of his eyes flashed. Sam kept the soft bristles against his scars. If she didn't show Blue she was higher up in the herd than him she'd never earn his respect.

Sam counted to ten before moving the brush to his neck and stroking his hide. After the horse relaxed, she repeated the process and placed the brush against the scars on his chest. Blue made no threatening movement and Sam rewarded him with several love pats before she put the brush back in the grooming belt. "Good boy, Blue. That's enough for now."

Proud of herself for sticking to her guns she cut through the middle of the paddock toward the gate. She wasn't sure what made her glance over her shoulder but when she did, she darn near fainted. Blue pawed the dirt, snorted and charged.

Sam wasn't sure if it was sheer determination or stupidity that kept her from fleeing. Shoulders squared she thrust her arms out to her sides and waved them. "Stop!" she shouted, then stamped her foot.

Blue veered away at the last second, his tail slapping Sam across the face. Heart beating like a jackhammer she remained rooted to the spot, daring Blue to charge again. Sides heaving the gelding dropped his head and slowly walked toward her, then gently nudged her chest with his nose. Tears welled in Sam's eyes. Blue had conceded defeat. Dear, God, she'd won.

With shaky hands she stroked his nose. "I'll never hurt you, Blue." After a few more pats, Sam once again turned her back on the horse and walked to the gate. A docile Blue followed. Before she left the paddock she fished a carrot from her pocket. "You and I are going to be good friends, Blue."

"ARE YOU SURE MISS SAM WANTS us to go fishing with her, Dad?"

"Positive." Wade turned the BMW onto the freshly graded and graveled road leading to the Peterson farm. Samantha had phoned his office and invited him and Luke out to the property Saturday to fish and picnic. Even though the weather forecast predicted late-afternoon thunderstorms, Wade had jumped at the chance to do something other than shovel dirt on his day off. And spending time with Samantha was hardly a chore.

Wade had used the long drive to the ranch to rehearse what he'd say to Samantha about her trust fund. He'd carried a hefty load of guilt on his shoulder since their lunch this past Wednesday.

He was ashamed to admit Samantha's kiss at Beulah's had caught him off guard and derailed his confession. Part of him was glad he hadn't been forthright with her. He cared for Samantha and he admitted he'd gotten a little cocky when he'd realized she was attracted to him. The fact that she was nice to Luke and that his son liked Samantha, too, had Wade contemplating the future. He hadn't been looking for a serious relationship when Samantha exploded into his life but now he had trouble picturing a future without her. He knew if they were to have a chance together he had to fess up.

"Did you tell her we can't fish?" Luke squinted out the window.

"I forgot."

"She's gonna guess when we get our lines tangled."

"Maybe Samantha will give us a few pointers and we'll do better."

Wade parked next to the corrals, well away from the construction crew hard at work putting the finishing touches on the new barn.

"Look, Dad." Luke pointed to a brand-new single-wide trailer sitting near the decrepit farmhouse.

"Must belong to one of the workers." He hoped so. He'd cashed in a CD to pay for the barn. He prayed by the time Samantha decided whether to demolish the farmhouse or renovate the place he'd have recovered her money.

Speaking of money... Damn his uncle. The man hadn't returned Wade's calls. Wade had questioned the firm's top executives about the company's investment activities, but the employees insisted they knew nothing about Charles's recent actions.

"How big do you think the fish are?" Luke unsnapped his seat belt.

"Why don't you ask Miss Samantha? She's headed our way." Wade stepped from the car, his eyes soaking up the vision marching toward them. Today her long ponytail poked out the back of a Sooners baseball cap. Her tight jeans had holes in the knees and a faded Sooners T-shirt clung to her curves.

"Hey, guys. Glad you could make it." She ruffled Luke's hair.

"You went to college at the University of Oklahoma?" Wade gestured to the logo on her T-shirt.

"No, my brother Matt did."

Wade wanted to ask what college she'd attended but Luke interrupted. "Where are we gonna fish, Miss Sam?"

"There's a pond on the other side of the property. Millicent's packing our lunch." Samantha slid Luke's glasses up his nose. "Why don't you see if she needs help."

As soon as Luke was out of earshot, Wade nodded to the trailer. "What's this?"

"My new home."

"You bought the trailer for yourself?"

"I got a smokin' deal on it." She chuckled. "My father's high-school classmate owns an RV dealership."

"What kind of smokin' deal?" Wade braced himself, praying he wouldn't have to put his condo on the market and move into the local YMCA before this ordeal with Samantha's trust fund was resolved.

"I got it for free."

"Free?" She had to be pulling his leg.

"It's a showroom trailer. Mr. Henderson said I could borrow it as long as I needed."

The tight band around Wade's chest loosened. "They're making good progress on the barn."

She snapped her fingers. "I forgot to mention at lunch the other day—"

That dreaded word *forgot* set off warning bells in Wade's head.

"—next on my to-do list is the old barn. The construction crew's returning next week to begin repairs on that, so I'll have additional storage for feed and equipment."

If you don't tell her about her missing trust fund she won't stop with the renovations.

"How many horses do you intend to take in?"

Coward.

"Three to begin with." Her smile rivaled the hot noon sun. "My favorite of the group is Blue. He's a twenty-year-old gray Arabian." She motioned to her temporary home. "That's why I had the trailer delivered. Once the barn is ready the SPCA will bring the horses."

A burning sensation erupted in Wade's chest. He felt as if he was running from an avalanche, trying to keep ahead of the fast-moving snow but losing ground with each step. "I like the baseball cap," he said, silently cursing. The compliment hadn't come out the way he'd intended. He'd meant to say she looked especially pretty today.

"Thanks." She wiggled the toe of her boot in the dirt, and he wondered if she'd thought about their kiss at Beulah's as much as he had. Before the strain became unbearable, Millicent and Luke emerged from the shanty.

"Would you mind bringing Millicent's rocking chair along?" Samantha asked.

"Sure." Wade dragged the heavy oak chair to the truck, then lifted it into the bed. Samantha added a picnic basket and Wade fetched the cooler of drinks he'd volunteered to bring.

Millicent and Luke sat in the backseat, and Wade joined Samantha in the front. Instead of driving to the main road, Samantha turned the truck around and headed past the old barn where she picked up a dirt trail barely wide enough to accommodate the truck. After a mile of bumping along, she said, "The pond's beyond that grouping of trees ahead."

Samantha stopped the truck at the top of an incline that overlooked a small oasis in the middle of dry, dusty farmland. An ancient tree towered among smaller oaks encircling a pond the size of an Olympic-size swimming pool. Clumps of wildflowers grew along the water's edge and shade dotted the sparse grass beneath the trees.

"Where does the water supply come from?" he asked.

"A natural spring." Samantha drove forward a few yards, then parked.

Interesting. The drilling company Wade called had

insisted the water table sat several hundred feet below-ground. Wade would have wasted Samantha's money if not for Millicent's water-witching talents. For the life of him, he couldn't understand why Samantha hadn't told him about the pond's existence. Had he been aware of the natural spring, he'd have challenged the drilling company's quote and possibly received a lower bid, sparing him sore muscles and blisters from hours of digging.

Then you wouldn't have had an excuse to spend the weekends with Samantha.

"What kind of fish are we gonna catch, Miss Sam?" Luke hopped out of the backseat.

"Bluegill and sunfish." Samantha helped Millicent out of the truck.

"Caught me a bluegill last week," the old woman boasted. She placed her bony hand on Luke's shoulder. "Ever skinned a fish?"

"Nope."

"Ya best catch one so I can show ya how it's done."

Luke removed his shoes and poked his toes in the water while Wade dragged Millicent's rocking chair to the edge of the pond, then repositioned it three times until the old woman was satisfied with the spot. Samantha spread a quilt beneath the trees and Wade set the picnic basket and cooler at opposite corners to prevent the blanket from blowing away.

After Samantha and Wade unloaded the fishing gear, Millicent was the first to cast her line across the pond, while Samantha showed Luke how to bait a hook.

"Yuck." Luke pinched the end of his nose when Samantha removed the lid from a shallow plastic dish.

"Stink bait," she said. "And these are nightcrawlers." She popped the lid off another container.

"They're still alive," Luke protested.

"That's because the fish won't bite if they're not wiggling on the hook. Which bait do you want to use?"

"A worm."

Wade grinned at his son's less-than-enthusiastic response. Once Samantha had the worm on the hook, she adjusted the tension on the line and handed the pole to Luke, and he cast the line.

"Good job. Now hold the pole steady." His son beamed under Samantha's praise. "That's perfect. If you feel a tug on the line give a shout." She moved sideways, bumping Wade. "Sorry."

"She fell asleep." He motioned to Millicent.

"Wait until a fish tugs on the line." Samantha smiled affectionately at the old woman. "She'll pop out of the chair like a jack-in-the-box."

Wade studied Samantha's profile, awed by her beauty. He wanted to slip off the baseball cap and free her hair from the elastic band. Then bury his face in the soft strands.

"Wade?"

He shook his head to declutter his brain. "What?"

"Let's sit in the shade."

More than happy to oblige, he followed her to the blanket. "How's your father taking the news of your plans?" He stretched out alongside her.

"Better than I expected."

She didn't elaborate, but he suspected Dominick Cartwright had strongly objected. Wade admired Samantha for standing up to her father. He wanted to ask about her relationship with Dominick but worried the topic would lead to a conversation about her trust fund, which he intended to bring up at the end of the picnic.

"May I ask you a personal question?" She fluttered her long, dark lashes.

"Sure."

"Why did you divorce Luke's mother?"

The blood in his veins cooled and Wade swung his gaze to the pond. He wasn't opposed to discussing his marriage to Carmen, but he feared he might come up short in Samantha's eyes.

"Carmen is the daughter of one of the firm's clients. We were introduced at a business meeting." Wade was ashamed to admit he'd been sucked in by Carmen's pretty face and flattering attention. What he hadn't discovered until too late was that his wife lost interest in people quickly. Wade had had the unfortunate luck of being transferred to Carmen's been-there-done-that list not too long after tying the knot. "When Luke was born Carmen handed over the child-rearing duties to me and various housekeepers."

"Not all women are cut out to be mothers," Samantha said.

She sounded defensive and he wondered if she didn't care for the idea of motherhood, either. He must have misinterpreted her reaction. Samantha was too patient and kind with Luke to not want to be a mother.

"When our relationship deteriorated," Wade continued, "I kept hoping things would improve, but the truth was Carmen had become bored with our marriage."

The corner of Samantha's mouth curved. "You're kidding, right?"

"I'm serious."

Samantha collapsed on the blanket and giggled.

"What's so funny?" Resting on his elbow, he leaned closer.

Splotches of red appeared on her cheeks. "I think you're plenty exciting," she whispered. "I'm never bored when I'm with you."

His ego inflated, threatening to burst. He brushed his lips across Samantha's. He would have pulled away but her hand snuck around his neck, keeping his mouth against her.

Lips caressed. Tongues played. Hot…heavy…

"I caught a fish!" Luke shouted.

Samantha sprang from the blanket and sprinted to the edge of the pond. Wade stayed behind, willing his body to cool off.

"Look, Dad. Miss Sam says it's a bluegill." Luke held up the fishing line.

"Congratulations!" Wade discreetly adjusted his pants and joined the duo at the pond.

"Now it's your father's turn," Samantha said, her gaze pinning him. "Maybe he'll get lucky and catch… something."

Or someone.

Chapter Eleven

"Will Luke be okay with Millicent?" Wade asked, staring out the window of Samantha's trailer. The torrential downpour had turned the ranch yard into a mud bog.

With each passing second Sam's hopes for a romantic evening were fading. "They'll be fine," she said. As for her and Wade... Since they'd entered the trailer, he'd paced the small enclosure like a caged animal searching for an escape route.

"That shack probably leaks like a sieve," he grumbled.

Swallowing a sigh, she peered out the window. "Barney nailed down new shingles not long ago."

"What if the storm worsens?"

Sam swallowed sigh number two. She'd flipped on the weather radio when they'd returned from fishing and learned the severe storms had passed west of the area. Already the rain had eased up. "Sky's clearing."

Wade stopped at her side. "There could be another line of storms following this one." He tilted his head, bringing their faces closer—dark lashes blinked behind his glasses.

A pang sliced through Sam, and she backed away.

She hadn't set out to seduce Wade, but Millicent had handed her a gift when the old woman had suggested Luke spend the night with her learning how to clean and smoke fish. Meanwhile Sam wanted Wade to stay with her—preferably in her bed.

But he appeared determined to thwart her plans. Maybe that was best. There could be no future with Wade. Why deepen a relationship that would end before ever getting off the ground?

Because Wade's special and you're falling in love with him.

Sam should have guarded her heart more closely around Wade, but she hadn't the energy or willpower to deny herself the pleasure of being with him. Wade made her feel alive again. He was good for her ego, good for her self-esteem…just plain good for her.

"We should have returned to Tulsa after the first downpour," he said.

Frustrated, Sam set about tidying the kitchen. The group had arrived at the trailer before the first rain shower and instead of the cookout she'd planned, they'd eaten boiled hot dogs. A break in the weather followed an hour of board games, then Luke and Millicent had dodged puddles to her cabin.

"Kind of crowded in here," Wade muttered.

Okay. She got the message. Nothing was going to happen between them tonight. The signals had been there earlier in the afternoon but Sam had chosen to ignore them—Wade had enjoyed the picnic at the pond, but he'd been agitated. "Is something on your mind?" She was more than happy to lend an ear if he wished to talk.

His eyes widened and she swore his expression mirrored shock. "No. Why?"

She shrugged. "You've been distracted all day." Now that she considered it, he'd cast her several worried glances since the rain had begun.

"A lot's going on at work," he said.

So much for believing they'd grown close in such a short time. Throat tight, Sam stowed the Monopoly game in a cupboard. "I'm taking a quick shower, then I might read before turning out the lights."

The gusty breath Wade blew out felt like a slap across the cheek.

Nightshirt and a clean pair of panties in hand, she slipped into the bathroom where she showered in record time, refusing to linger under the warm spray or she'd give in to the temptation to cry. Since meeting Wade her emotions had undergone an Olympic workout and right now she hadn't the strength for more disappointment.

After shutting off the water she towel-dried and slipped into the nightshirt. She dabbed on face cream, brushed her teeth, then ran a comb through her tangled hair. *Don't be a quitter.*

The stubborn streak she'd inherited from her father surfaced and she decided to try one more time for a romantic evening. She paused outside the bathroom door. "Wade, what do you say I make hot chocolate and we watch…" He'd fallen asleep on the sofa bed. She tiptoed closer, gently removed his glasses and placed them on the counter.

With a heavy heart she retreated to the bedroom.

If she was lucky maybe she and Wade would go all the way in her dreams.

WADE AWOKE IN THE MIDDLE of the night, hot and… *bothered?* The last remnants of his erotic dream, starring Samantha, faded, leaving him rock-hard and irritable. He swung his feet to the floor and groaned when his back muscles protested. He'd have been better off sleeping on the hard ground than the camping mattress on the pullout bed. The blurry glow of the microwave clock reminded him he wasn't wearing his glasses. He patted the countertop until his fingers bumped the frames. He slipped them on, waited for his eyes to adjust, then wondered what the hell he was going to do at 1:00 a.m. in the morning.

Might as well take a shower and cool off. He snuck into the bathroom, stepped inside the stall, flipped the faucet to cold and soaped himself. The tepid water did little to relieve his arousal. Frustrated, he dried off, tied the towel around his hips and opened the bathroom door. Then froze.

What was that?

A sniffle? He inched toward Samantha's bedroom door and held his breath. More sniffling. Had she come down with a cold?

Don't be an ass. She's crying.

He rested his forehead against the door and closed his eyes. He hadn't meant to hurt her. A short while ago he'd yearned to make love as badly as she'd wanted to. He'd rejoiced that such a beautiful, sweet woman desired him. But his conscience had gotten the best of him. He didn't dare make love when he hadn't been truthful about her trust fund. Right or wrong, the blame for her missing money rested squarely on his shoulders—at least until he proved otherwise.

Her money isn't the only thing holding you back.

He had a responsibility to his son. The divorce hadn't been easy on Luke. If Wade and Samantha entered into a serious relationship, he wouldn't be able to prevent Luke from becoming more attached to Samantha than he already was, especially when the boy's own mother showed little interest in him. If things didn't work out between Wade and Samantha then Luke's heart would be broken.

What about your heart?

Wade admitted that his feelings for Samantha had moved past attraction. Past a sense of concern for her horse sanctuary and the trust fund. Past wanting to impress her. To make her happy. Wade had fallen in love with her.

Another sniffle echoed behind the door. To hell with telling her the truth about her missing money. To hell with his worry over Luke becoming too attached to Samantha. To hell with Wade's heart falling in love with the wealthy cowgirl. He had to end Samantha's tears. He rapped his knuckles against the bedroom door.

"Wh-what is it?" she sputtered.

He tested the knob, found it unlocked and poked his head around the doorframe. The bedside lamp cast a warm glow around the room. Samantha sat in the middle of the mattress, legs tucked to the side, her long, dark hair falling over her shoulders in disarray. Her nightshirt clung to her breasts, outlining their shape and fullness. Her legs were bare except for the scrap of pink lace peeking out from beneath the hem of the shirt.

"Sorry I woke you." She wiped her swollen eyes with the back of her hand and offered a brave smile.

Her apology made his heart ache. Without considering the consequences he entered her room and shut the door, then leaned against it. "You should be sorry," he said. The tiny catch in her breath excited him. "I've been dreaming about you."

The tears stopped and Wade relaxed. "And this is what dreaming of you does to me." Praying he wasn't about to make a fool of himself, he loosened the knot at his waist and the towel fell to the floor.

Her gaze zeroed in on his rock-hard erection and he froze. Did he pounce? Did he ask permission? *Help me, Samantha.*

She came to his rescue, whipping the T-shirt over her head and flinging it across the room. Golden skin, round breasts and legs that went on forever—the real thing was far better than his fantasy. She shifted to her knees and held out her hand, beckoning.

An electric shock leapt up his arm when she placed his hand over her heart and lifted her face, seeking a kiss. Unable to deny her anything, he kissed her, showing her how much she meant to him. How much he wanted to please her. To rock her world.

"You're incredibly beautiful." He toyed with the scrap of lace clinging to her hips, his fingers stroking the soft skin. "Inside and out." He pressed a light kiss to her bare shoulder.

Her smile eased the nervous tension in his gut and he stretched out next to her on the mattress. She shimmied out of her panties, then removed his glasses. "Wait." He grasped her hand. "I'm blind as a bat without them."

Snuggling closer, she purred, "Then you'll just have

to feel your way around." She dropped the glasses on the nightstand.

His senses kicked into high gear—her tantalizing scent teased his nose. Her velvety skin burned his fingertips. Her soft sighs serenaded his ears. And her sweet taste filled his mouth.

Time froze as their fingers tormented and teased. Mouths feasted. He ignored his building desire, focusing on Samantha, ensuring his kiss, his touch drove her higher and higher until…

Samantha shuddered, and moaned, then curled into Wade and sighed. "That was incredible."

If he'd been a rooster he'd have strutted atop the mattress.

"Your turn." She sprawled across his chest.

"I don't have any protection with me," he confessed. After their first kiss on the porch swing Wade had considered stashing a condom in his wallet but had felt foolish at the idea, because he'd never expected—wished for—but never expected that they'd reach this moment.

"I have a condom in my purse."

Did she always carry birth control in her purse? Or did she…

"I've wanted to make love with you since the day you helped dig the well." She kissed him, her tongue sweeping across his teeth.

"Really?"

"Yep." Another kiss. More tongue.

"Ah, Sam," he whispered.

"It's about time you called me Sam."

"The condoms…" He was ready to explode.

She crawled over him, hopped off the bed and

rummaged through her purse, offering him a sweet albeit blurry view of her shapely backside. "Oh, good," she said.

"What?"

"I've got three." Then she pounced. Limbs tangled and heartbeats thundered. With slow, steady strokes he loved her, carrying them higher, cloud by cloud until they vaulted into the heavens among an explosion of stars.

AT 3:00 A.M. SAM AWOKE shivering, the air conditioner blasting her naked body. She tugged the bedcovers up, then spooned Wade, pressing her breasts to his back and wiggling her foot between his calves. Then she rubbed her nose in the curve of his neck and breathed in his masculine scent.

Making love with Wade had been incredible. His caresses, kisses and murmured endearments had melted her heart. In the aftermath of their lovemaking, while they'd struggled to catch their breath, Sam realized that Wade had been the first man she'd allowed herself to lose control with. She only wished this magical *whatever* that was happening between them had somewhere to go. She might wish for a long-term relationship with Wade but sweet little Luke stood in the way. She doubted Wade would entrust her with his son's safety once he learned another child had almost died in her care.

What if Wade trusts you with his son and still wants to keep seeing you?

There was a small part of Sam that wondered if maybe with the help of a considerate man she could be a good mother. What if the memory lapses miraculously disappeared when she had to safeguard her own child?

She'd never know, because she refused to risk a child's well-being for her own happiness.

Sam would always be a liability in any relationship that involved a child. Her heart believed Wade would view her memory lapses and forgetfulness as minor inconveniences—until catastrophe struck, forcing him to choose his son over her. Sam intended to be grateful for these precious few moments with Wade and pray the memories were enough to last through her lifetime.

WADE GROANED AS SAMANTHA rubbed her luscious body against his backside. She'd blown him away with her enthusiasm in bed. Her soft sighs, lusty stares and bold touches made him feel like the king of kings. The world's greatest lover. The Don Juan of rodeo cowboys. When Wade was with Samantha he forgot he wore glasses. Forgot he didn't sport bulging muscles or walk with a swagger.

He wanted more.

Rolling to his back he curled his arm around Samantha and she snuggled closer, resting her cheek against his heart. The simple gesture made his throat swell. No need for words or confessions—they both understood they'd crossed a line they could never erase.

If only he'd been forthright with her from the beginning. He feared that after he revealed the firm had lost her money—make that *he* had lost her money—she'd accuse him of seducing her to smooth things over.

Tell her now. He would. As soon as she…

Samantha's mouth traveled at alarming speed down his chest, across his stomach, over his hips and…oh, man. A few more seconds of her attention and Wade was on the verge of losing control. He reversed their positions, fumbled for a condom on the nightstand, then sheathed himself and slid inside her.

The notion that this gorgeous woman wanted *him*— Wade Dawson—drove him closer to the edge. He slowed the pace of their lovemaking, wanting to savor these moments, afraid of what would happen when they were both back in the real world.

Slow gave way to fast. The kisses grew wild, hot. The touches explosive as they raced to the finish line.

They floated back to earth to the quiet hum of the air conditioner. Their bodies, slick with perspiration, stuck together. Wade didn't care. He would have lain with Samantha forever if his cell phone hadn't gone off in the other room. "I'd better answer it." He untangled their limbs and rolled out of bed. "Hello?"

"We've had a hell of a time connecting."

Thank God his uncle had called. Tired of playing tag, Wade cut to the chase. "Where are you?"

"Mexico."

"We need to talk."

"I'm arriving in Tulsa on Monday. I'll see you at the office."

"You'd better be there or I'm handling this my way," Wade threatened.

His uncle cleared his throat. "Not a word to anyone until we speak." *He disconnected.*

"What's wrong?" Samantha stood in the doorway, wrapped in the bedsheet. Hair mussed. Mouth swollen. Heavy-lidded eyes begged him to make love to her again.

"Nothing." Another lie. He'd examine his guilty

feelings later, not now. "My uncle's returning from an overseas business trip on Monday." He traced the curve of her jaw with one finger. "Now, where were we?"

She batted her eyelashes. "Want me to show you?"

He grinned. "Lead the way."

A KNOCK ON THE TRAILER DOOR awoke Sam from a dead sleep. She bolted upright and searched for Wade—his side of the bed was empty. And cold.

"Good morning, buddy."

"Hi, Dad. Where's Miss Sam?"

Samantha's heart warmed at the sound of Luke's voice.

"She's sleeping," Wade said.

"Can I eat breakfast here?"

"Sure. Is Millicent joining us?"

"She made grits but I didn't like them, so she told me to go eat with you guys in the trailer."

Cupboard doors opened and closed. "How about cereal?"

"What kind?"

"Frosted Flakes."

"Okay."

Sam leaned against the headboard and continued eavesdropping on the two males.

"How'd you sleep last night?" Wade asked.

"Okay, I guess. Millicent doesn't sleep."

"What do you mean?"

"I woke up to go to the bathroom and she was sitting in her rocking chair in the dark."

"Lots of old people snooze in chairs."

"She wasn't snoozing, Dad. She was talking out loud."

"To who?"

"A ghost."

Oh, dear. Sam forgot about Millicent's midnight chats with her deceased husband. Time to come out of hiding before Wade got worked up over nothing. She dressed quickly—a shower would have to wait—and padded barefoot into the kitchen area. "Good morning, gentlemen." She took a bowl from the cupboard and joined them at the table.

"Hi, Miss Sam. Did you know Millicent talks to ghosts?"

Her gaze collided with Wade's and her breath caught at the warmth in his eyes. "She's not talking to just any ghost," she answered Luke. "Millicent converses with her husband."

"Didn't you say he died in the war?" Wade's attention shifted to the front of her blouse and Sam's breathing escalated.

"He did." Fearing she'd launch herself into Wade's arms if she didn't get a hold of her emotions, she trained her eyes on Luke. "When an old person lives by themselves for a long time they become lonely. Millicent understands her husband is dead but she's comforted by believing his spirit lives with her in the cabin."

"I was right, Dad. Millicent talks to ghosts." Luke shoveled a spoonful of cereal into his mouth. "What are we gonna do today?"

"Don't speak with your mouth full," Wade scolded. "We're heading back to the condo. You have homework to finish and I have business calls to make."

The last traces of euphoria from their night of love-making evaporated at Wade's statement. Sam wasn't ready to say goodbye to the Dawson males. "How would you both like to see one of the horses coming to live at the ranch?"

"Cool! Can we, Dad?"

"The horse you've been working with at the SPCA?" Wade asked.

"His name's Blue." She smiled at Luke. "I'm eager to see how he reacts to children."

"Let's go see Blue, Dad."

Sam offered her sweetest smile, drawing Wade's gaze to her mouth. His eyes softened and she knew he was recalling their lovemaking. *Please, Wade. Give us a little more time together.*

"Why not," he said.

Samantha's spirits soared. "Let me grab a quick shower and then we'll leave." She disappeared into the bathroom before Wade could change his mind.

THE SPCA STABLES IMPRESSED Wade and surprised him at the same time. He had no idea there were so many horses in need of rescuing. Samantha introduced him to Nancy Parker, the facility manager, and after giving the group a quick tour, she left them watching the horses in the paddocks.

"Ready to feed Blue a carrot?" Samantha asked Luke.

"Sure." Luke followed her to the horse.

Wade stayed out of the way, pleased by his son's show of enthusiasm for an activity that didn't involve schoolwork.

"She's doing great, isn't she?" Nancy Parker stopped at Wade's side.

"Samantha you mean?"

The stable manager nodded. "She's worked with the horses for months and has come a long way."

Wade wasn't following the conversation. "Samantha's been around horses all her life, hasn't she?"

"After the injury she suffered in high school, she's had nothing to do with horses. Until a few months ago. I was surprised and pleased to hear she intended to open a sanctuary ranch." Nancy motioned to a truck and horse trailer entering through the facility's main gate. "That's our new boarder. Gotta go."

Wade studied Samantha with a critical eye, searching for signs of fear or trepidation as she and Luke petted Blue. He saw only confidence and self-assurance. And what injury had the SPCA manager been referring to? He hadn't noticed any scars or evidence of old wounds when he'd made love to Samantha. The incident with the horse must have been a minor mishap or she'd have told him.

Just because the two of you made love doesn't mean you're privy to all her secrets. But he wanted to be.

Wade's cell phone vibrated in his pocket. He checked the number and grimaced. "Hello, Carmen."

"I realize this is short notice," Wade's ex-wife said, "but I need you to keep Luke tonight. He doesn't have summer-school classes tomorrow because of a teacher seminar."

"Why can't you watch him?" No way was Wade missing the meeting with his uncle.

"A fabulous opportunity came along. Remember my friend Sherri?"

No.

"Her husband's cousin married the daughter of Senator Lewis. Anyway, Sherri invited me to attend a luncheon for the senator's wife and everybody that's anybody in Tulsa will be there. I simply can't miss it."

Wade allowed his gaze to wander to Samantha and Luke. His son acted more at ease with Samantha than he did with his own mother. If he told Carmen no, she'd simply hire a sitter and go to the luncheon anyway. "Fine. I'll keep Luke with me and see that he gets to school Tuesday morning."

"Thanks for being such a dear. Give Luke my love. Bye."

That was him all right—*a dear.* Wade wondered how long he'd be able to protect his son from figuring out he wasn't his mother's top priority. He headed toward the duo, hoping to convince Samantha to allow Luke to spend the day with her tomorrow.

Chapter Twelve

"C'mon, Luke. We're heading out to buy feed for the horses." Sam signaled to the construction foreman that she was leaving. The crew had arrived earlier in the morning to finish installing the doors on the horse stalls inside the new steel barn.

Sam ruffled Luke's hair as they headed toward her truck. She'd suffered a mini heart attack yesterday when Wade had asked if his son could spend today with her while he worked at Dawson Investments. Sam's ears had rung and she'd barely heard Wade's explanation about his wife having a prior commitment and Monday being a summer-school holiday. Backed into a corner, Sam had agreed.

How could she have said no without giving a reason why? Sam refused to mention her cognitive shortfalls— not when her and Wade's relationship had moved from professional to friends to friends with bedroom privileges. Besides, she was all about facing her fears now. She *could* be responsible for a child.

"Hop in the backseat and buckle up, kiddo."

"Where are we going?"

"To Barney's." The old man never took advantage of Sam's forgetfulness and she rewarded his loyalty by purchasing goods at his store, even though his prices were much higher than the bigger chains.

"Who's Barney?" Luke asked.

Did all high-IQ kids ask so many questions? "Barney runs a business that sells feed and supplies to ranches and farms in this area. His grandfather opened the store years ago."

"Why are you buying feed when you don't have any horses?"

"Remember the nice lady you met at the SPCA yesterday? She needs me to take Blue so she can use his stall for another horse they're rescuing."

"Blue's coming today?"

"Yep."

"Cool."

Sam answered Luke's questions until she pulled into the parking lot of the feed store. When they entered the building a gruff "Who's there?" greeted them.

Luke edged closer to Sam. "He sounds grumpy."

"Grumpier 'n a one-eyed cat." Barney stepped into the open, face twisted in a grimace.

"Barney, shame on you." Sam patted Luke's shoulder. "This is Mr. Barney, Luke. Barney, this is Wade Dawson's son. He's my sidekick for the day."

"Don't look like no sidekick I ever seen."

Eyes narrowed, Sam studied the boy's button-down short-sleeved shirt and khaki shorts—a bit wrinkled and dirty after having been worn two days in a row. "You're right, Barney. Luke needs cowboy duds if he's going to work with horses."

Eyes bright with excitement, Luke asked, "I get to dress like a real cowboy?"

"I reckon that's what she's tellin' ya, kid." Barney motioned for the boy to follow him. "C'mon. I'll show ya the cowboy gear."

When they stopped at a table piled high with jeans, Sam removed the list of items she'd written. "I'll be needing these supplies."

"Sure thing." Barney shuffled into the storeroom.

Sam eyeballed Luke's frame, then dug through the children's jeans, found a pair his size and held them up to his waist. "Those should work." Next, she moved to the dusty circular rack of children's western-style shirts. She selected a long-sleeved blue cotton shirt with miniature brown horses galloping across the front. "Now for a pair of boots."

"Over there." Luke raced across the store where boxes of boots lined the wall. "They're all too big."

"Junior boots are at the end." After perusing sizes, she chose a pair of black Ropers. "Take a seat on the stool."

Luke tugged off his sneakers. Sam helped him with the boots—too big. The next—too small. The third…

"Good enough."

"Can I wear all this stuff right now?"

"Sure. There's a dressing room over there." She pointed to the wooden door a few feet away. Five minutes later the boy wore a huge grin.

"You look like a cowpoke, Luke," Sam said.

He stomped his boot. "You think Blue will know I'm not a real cowboy?"

"Not if you're wearing a hat." She held out her hand and Luke slipped his fingers through hers.

The hat selection consisted of straw hats—best for hot summer months. "What color do you prefer?"

Luke tried on black, red and brown. "Black," he said.

"Black it is." She tilted the hat a bit forward on his head. "Perfect." Out of the corner of her eye she spotted a red bandanna. Any cowpoke worth his salt carried a bandanna—whether to clean his six-shooter with, write a farewell letter to his lover on, or shine his boots with.

"Tommy done loaded the feed into the back of yer truck," Barney announced, when he emerged from the store room.

"Who's Tommy?" Luke asked.

"Tommy's my dumb-headed nephew who ain't got the brains of a jellyfish."

"Jellyfish don't have brains," Luke said. "And they're not really a fish. They don't have a head, heart, eyes, ears or even bones."

"Ya some walkin', talkin' encyclopedia, kid?" Barney grumbled.

"Luke's a smart young man," Sam boasted, tearing off the price tags from Luke's new clothes and setting them on the counter. "Put it all on my tab and—"

"Yer personal money manager will pay the bill." Barney patted his pocket. "Got his card here somewhere."

"Thanks, Barney." Sam and Luke left. Not until she parked the truck at the ranch did she breathe a huge sigh of relief that nothing had happened to Luke during their outing. So far, so good.

Before she and Luke had finished unloading the supplies from the truck bed the SPCA trailer arrived with Blue and a second horse.

"Nancy didn't mention anything about taking Whisper today." Sam accepted the mare's reins from Ken, a stable hand at the SPCA.

"Nancy said they rescued a second horse from a ranch north of Tulsa and hoped you'd agree to keep the mare." Ken returned to the trailer and unloaded Blue. "Nancy said to tell you that Red's getting dropped off next week."

Sam unlatched the paddock gate and she and Ken walked the horse inside.

"Why do you call her Whisper?" Luke asked Ken.

"The mare had a throat infection when she arrived at the SPCA and she neighed so softly you could hardly hear. Now that she's recovered, she makes more noise than a barn full of donkeys."

Sam rubbed the mare's nose, patted Blue's neck, then left the paddock and locked the gate latch behind her.

Luke strutted over to the fence and stood on the lower rung. The kid hadn't stopped preening since the workmen in the barn made a big deal over the boy's new duds.

Sam signed the paperwork, then thanked Ken before he drove off.

"Can I pet Whisper?" Luke asked.

"I'm not sure—" His disappointed face tugged at Sam's heart. He'd been such a trooper all day—not a word of complaint, even agreeing to eat a granola bar for lunch because she hadn't had time to cook anything. "Be right back." Lead rope in hand, she entered the corral and approached Whisper. "It's okay, girl. I won't hurt you." The mare lowered her head and snuffled. Sam rubbed her neck before clipping the rope to the halter. She rewarded Whisper's cooperation with a sugar cube from her pocket. "Let's make another friend, shall we?" She led the mare to Luke, who'd climbed to the top rung of the corral.

"Hold your palm out flat and let her sniff."

Luke followed Sam's instructions, giggling when Whisper's nose tickled his skin. "Now gently pat the side of her neck." Sam placed Luke's hand on the mare's hide.

"Hi, Whisper. Miss Sam's gonna take real good care of you. I promise."

Whisper backed up, a signal she'd had enough affection. Sam released the lead rope. "Good girl." The mare trotted off to the feed bin. "C'mon, Luke. We've got work to do in the barn."

Once inside the new structure Sam gave the boy several chores to keep him busy while she prepared a stall for Whisper. She whistled as she went to work, her confidence growing by the minute. She had no doubt her sanctuary ranch would flourish and she'd prove to herself and others that Samantha Cartwright was capable of managing her own life.

What could possibly go wrong?

"YOU LIED TO ME," WADE SAID as he waltzed into his uncle's office.

"Shut the door. I don't want anyone overhearing this conversation."

Wade obliged, then sat in the chair facing the mahogany desk, which looked like a prop used in a play—standard pencil holder, yellow legal pad, telephone, Rolodex and computer monitor. Nothing personal such as family photos, soda cans or sticky notes cluttered the surface.

"Samantha Cartwright's trust fund has been invested in a real estate deal that—" his uncle rubbed his brow "—to put it bluntly failed."

Wade attempted to voice a protest, but his uncle sliced a hand through the air, cutting him off. "Unforeseen circumstances led to several investors backing out at the eleventh hour. We hadn't anticipated any opposition and unfortunately we'd already invested Samantha's entire savings in the project."

"Since when does Dawson Investments deal in real estate?" And why hadn't Wade been informed of the company's new venture? Samantha's account was *his* to manage, not his uncle's.

"You know very well that we don't invest our clients' money in real estate. But an extraordinary opportunity arose that I couldn't pass up."

"What you've done is unethical. And illegal."

"Don't act so righteous, Wade. If things would have worked out the way they should have the entire company, including your client, would have reaped the rewards."

"But it failed and Dawson Investments' reputation has been compromised." Wade slammed his fist on his uncle's desk, startling the old man. "How do you plan to recoup Samantha's losses?"

"There is no plan. Her money was used to purchase the island."

"What island?"

"In the United Arab Emirates. You may have heard of the famous Palm Islands—eighth wonder of the world?"

"Go on."

"Sheikh Mohammed bin Rashid Al Maktoum is determined to keep Dubai's reputation as one of the best tourist destinations, so he proposed the idea of creating several man-made islands that would support luxury hotels, residential villas and shoreline apartments off the coast of the emirate of Dubai." His uncle left his chair to stare out the office's floor-to-ceiling windows. "One of the sheikh's plans is to build three hundred islands in the shape of the world map. Our firm joined with other investors and purchased one of the few remaining islands for sale."

"What went wrong?" Wade forced himself to concentrate, determined to control his emotions so he didn't miss crucial information that might be used to help recover Samantha's money.

"Our partners got nervous when the U.S. economy faltered and they walked away from the deal."

"They didn't lose a dime, did they?" Wade said.

His uncle returned to his desk. "I've got my top executives searching for new investors, but no one's taking risks right now."

Wade didn't miss the emphasis on the word *top*. If working shady deals was a prerequisite to acquiring an executive position at his uncle's firm, then Wade had a lot of mulling over to do once the dust settled from this mess. "Did you use any other clients' funds to invest in this project?"

"No."

"Why Samantha Cartwright's money?" There were other clients' portfolios that rivaled hers.

"Because I never expected she'd demand her money on her thirty-second birthday."

"Why not?"

"For obvious reasons. Dominick's hovered over her since the accident and—"

"What accident are you referring to?" Everyone but Wade knew about the *accident.*

"You were in college at the time when Samantha was kicked in the head by a horse. I believe it happened shortly after we'd visited the ranch the summer she turned sixteen. She almost died." He shrugged as if the near-death experience had been nothing. "She was left with memory problems and difficulty concentrating. College was out of the question for her, so Dominick gave her a job in his company to make her feel useful."

Wade's mind grappled with the new information. Images flew through his head… All the notes Samantha wrote to herself. Her willingness to allow him to take over her finances without much of a fight. Her not remembering the tree-climbing incident when he'd visited the Lazy River.

"Dominick pays her a generous salary and she lives at home. Hell, there was never a need for her to withdraw any money from her trust fund."

"Well, you were wrong. She needs her money to turn a ranch she purchased into a horse sanctuary."

His uncle's eyes widened. "The girl's got grit, I'll give her that."

"What do you mean?"

"Rumor has it that Samantha's terrified of horses and hasn't ridden one since the accident."

Samantha had proved otherwise when they'd visited the horses at the SPCA yesterday. "She's overcome those fears." Wade admired her for it.

"Aren't you the least interested in knowing where

Samantha's obtaining the money to bankroll her new ranch?" When his uncle remained silent, Wade poked himself in the chest. "Me. I cashed in my 401(k) and used my savings to cover the expenses incurred thus far."

"If you receive the promotion you're in line for you'll recoup your money in bonuses."

"That's not the point," Wade argued. "What about next month's client financial statements? How do you plan to hide Samantha's losses?" Wade cringed when he imagined Dominick's reaction.

"We'll have to be creative for a while."

Wade was appalled his uncle would even consider mailing out falsified documents.

"This sanctuary ranch won't last," his uncle said. "Samantha's difficulty in focusing will cause her to lose interest quickly."

Lose interest? Wade's chest tightened when he envisioned how devastated she'd be if the ranch didn't succeed. He hated to see her dreams crushed because of his uncle's greed. Wade intended to make sure that didn't happen, starting with telling Samantha the truth. "I can't in good conscience keep this information from her." He'd waited far too long as it was and hoped—no, prayed—Samantha wouldn't send him packing—not after he'd gone and fallen in love with her.

His uncle chuckled. "Sounds as if you have a crush on the woman."

"My feelings for Samantha have nothing to do with telling her the truth. She's a client first and foremost and deserves a hell of a lot more honesty from her financial adviser than he's shown so far."

"Steer clear of her, Wade. Samantha's more trouble than she's worth. She's damaged goods. Even her fiancé could see that and he broke off their engagement."

The word *engagement* clanged inside Wade's head. Why hadn't Samantha mentioned she'd once been engaged? He felt foolish for having discussed his own failed marriage while she'd kept her past relationship a secret.

"Evidently the man left his child in Samantha's care and something happened to the kid."

His uncle's words didn't scare Wade. He knew deep down that Luke would be safe with Sam. He trusted her to take good care of his son. "My feelings for Samantha are none of your damned business. What matters is that Dominick Cartwright trusted Dawson Investments to safeguard his daughter's financial security and we— *you*—let him down."

"When I took you in years ago, Wade, I knew you were smart. You demonstrated that early on after you caught up in school and figured out how to deal with your dyslexia. But I see I've been remiss in teaching you something important about the business world."

"And what would that be?"

"Loyalty. There are times you don't question the motives or decisions of your superiors. You simply trust that they have the company's best interests at heart."

"Our loyalties should lie with our customers whose money allows us to prosper. Without them there would be no Dawson Investments."

"That's your mother in you talking, Wade. She was a pushover when it came to helping others. She believed she could change the world one lost soul at a time."

"What are you talking about?"

"Your father, of course."

"You've known all along who my father is?" If so, why hadn't his uncle come forward with the information when Wade had been a teenager and had asked about his birth father?

"Zeke was a handyman for the wealthy. If he had a last name he didn't share it with anyone. He painted our garage one summer and suckered your mother into sleeping with him."

"What does my father have to do with loyalty?"

"Zeke showed no allegiance toward your mother, leaving her to raise you alone until she died. Then that chore landed in my lap."

Chore? Nothing like being blunt.

"I had hoped you'd come to appreciate the opportunities and privileges you've received from the Dawson name."

"I'm grateful for what you've done for me." Wade darn near choked on the words.

"Then show me your gratitude by keeping your mouth shut."

Wade's blood boiled. "You're asking me to break the law."

There was an unnatural gleam in his uncle's eyes that Wade had never seen before. "If all goes as planned and we land another partner to invest in our island, Samantha stands to earn millions in profit and you'll receive all the credit." He grinned. "And a promotion to executive vice president."

A promotion in exchange for his silence. Wade felt

ill. All these years he'd believed he'd needed the title behind his name before he could leave his uncle's company to open his own investment firm. Now he had the opportunity to gain the title—but at what cost, his integrity? Or worse, his relationship with Samantha?

Wade's cell phone rang and he answered before checking the number. "Wade Dawson."

"Wade, you have to come out to the ranch right away." Samantha's panicked voice startled him.

"What's wrong?"

"It's Luke."

Heart pounding, he asked, "What happened?"

"He's missing."

"What do you mean, Luke's missing?"

"He was supposed to be helping me in the barn and I got distracted… I can't remember what I was doing, Wade." Her voice rose with each word. "When I checked on him, he was gone."

"I'm on my way." He snapped the phone shut and headed for the door.

"What happened?" his uncle asked.

"It's Luke. Samantha can't find him." Wade paused in the doorway—half of him needing to ask, the other half fearing the answer. "What happened to the child Samantha watched over?"

"I believe the little girl was bit by a snake."

"She survived, right?"

"Only because Dominick's pilot happened to be at the ranch that day and flew the girl by chopper to the emergency room in Tulsa."

Wade refused to allow his son to suffer a similar

fate. He took the stairs instead of the elevator and rushed from the building, his attention no longer focused on his uncle's shady business dealings, but on locating his son.

Chapter Thirteen

Dear God—it was happening all over again.

Shielding her eyes against the late-afternoon sun, Sam squinted into the distance. Nothing. Nothing but miles of red Oklahoma dirt.

"The boy ain't dumb. He'll make out okay 'til ya find him." Millicent's words fell far short of reassuring Sam. She and the old woman had scoured the ranch yard from top to bottom, then every nook and cranny in both barns and the trailer. They'd even checked beneath the tarp of Millicent's vintage car.

"Luuuke!" Sam shouted, the wind carrying his name off. She studied the dilapidated farmhouse. Had he gone inside to explore? Earlier in the morning while she and Luke had eaten breakfast she'd reviewed a list of ranch rules—do's and don'ts related to Luke's well-being and safety. The old farmhouse had been on the *don't* list.

Yesterday when Wade had asked her to watch Luke, Sam should have refused. But she'd wanted to prove to him and herself that she was capable of chaperoning his son. She'd failed miserably—again.

Please, God, let me find Luke before Wade arrives.

Her stomach churned, but Sam refused to succumb to the nausea. "I'm going inside the house." Millicent didn't protest, convincing Sam the old woman worried more than she let on.

Sam tiptoed around the collapsed porch steps and entered the house through the front door. She paused in the entry hall, listening for signs of movement. Nothing but wind whistled through the cracks and broken windows. "Luke, are you in here?" She edged toward the stairs, the warped wood floor squeaking beneath her feet.

Cold sweat—the kind spawned by uncontrollable fear—bubbled across her forehead. What if Luke had gone upstairs and had fallen and knocked himself unconscious? She tested the bottom step and her heart jumped inside her chest at the loud crack. Clutching the wobbly banister she climbed the stairs, counting each step—thirteen—until she reached the landing.

"Luke?" *Please answer.* She tiptoed toward the bedroom on her right. A single bed with an iron headboard and a yellow stained mattress occupied the room. The windows had been broken, fragments of glass sparkling in the sunlight that streamed across the floor. Cobwebs hung from the ceiling and animal droppings—probably mice—littered the floor. Sam crossed the room and peered inside a small closet. "Luke?"

No answer. Sam retreated from the room and headed down the hall. She glanced inside the bathroom on the way, wishing Luke had fallen asleep in the claw-foot tub, but the room was empty. When she twisted the knob on the second bedroom door, the hardware broke off in her hand. Using her shoulder she shoved the door open.

A putrid smell permeated the room—dead raccoon in the corner. This bedroom had no closet, leaving her one final place to check on the second floor—an attic storage compartment at the end of the hall. There was no sign of the boy in the small enclosure. Heart heavy she returned downstairs. When a thorough sweep of the first floor turned up no sign of Luke, Sam's throat swelled and her eyes burned.

Tears won't help.

"Sam!" Wade's shout startled her. She stumbled from the kitchen and met him at the front door.

The blasted tears she'd refused to shed spilled from her eyes. She opened her mouth to speak but to her horror the lump in her throat blocked the words.

Wade opened his arms and Sam flew into his embrace. She clung to him, her fingers digging into his back. "I'm sorry," she choked.

"Have you searched the entire ranch?" he asked, his voice hoarse with emotion.

"Yes."

He broke their embrace but kept his hands on her shoulders, and Sam was grateful for the warmth of his touch. "Did you check the barns?"

"Twice."

"Was there a construction crew here today?"

"Yes."

"Could one of the men have—"

"The workers left shortly after Luke and I returned from running errands. Luke was with me at the time."

"Let's get out of here before the roof caves in on our

heads." He slid his arm around her waist and half carried her down the rickety porch steps. When they rounded the corner of the house they bumped into Millicent.

Wade glanced between the two women. "Can you recall anything Luke said that might give a clue where—"

"That's the problem, Wade," Sam blurted. The anxiety bottled up inside her erupted. "I can't remember!" Lord help her, she was falling apart.

His eyes darkened with sympathy and for one horrifying moment she wondered if someone had told Wade about her memory troubles. "I made a list of things Luke wasn't allowed to do and we went over it this morning."

"Show me the list." Wade held out his hand.

Sam retrieved the crumpled yellow paper from her jean pocket.

"What's the witch's tower?" he asked.

An image of Luke, sunburned and dehydrated, flashed through Sam's mind. If the boy had taken off in search of the oil rig, he could have gotten lost, bitten by a snake or attacked by a coyote. "The witch's tower is an old wildcat well."

"Wildcat well?"

"They're small oil wells. The problem is they usually aren't capped properly because the speculators are flat broke by the time they abandon the site."

"What happens if the well's not capped?"

"If they fill the borehole in with dirt instead of cement, oil can leak out and pollute the water table." Samantha's head spun and she closed her eyes, fearing she might topple. "Or small animals and kids can fall in the borehole."

A gurgling noise erupted from Millicent's throat. "I told Luke 'bout the tower when we was fishin' at the pond the other day." Millicent wrung her knobby hands.

"Where's the rig?" Wade asked.

Sam pointed beyond the barns. "Over that rise in the distance."

"What about the pond? Maybe he went fishing?"

Sam had forgotten the pond. "I didn't check there."

"Let's split up. I'll drive to the pond. You head to the rig," Wade said.

"I'll find Luke. I promise," Sam pledged. The fastest way to reach the rig was by horse. She took off at a dead run for the barn. Wade returned to his car and sped away. Sam hadn't ridden a horse since her accident. The prospect terrified her as she stumbled to a halt in front of Blue's stall. She'd made tremendous progress with the gelding, but could she trust him to keep her safe long enough to find Luke?

Careful not to make any sudden moves that might startle Blue, she opened the stall door and stepped inside. After stroking the gelding's neck, the horse swung his head toward her and stared with his big brown eyes.

You have to help me, Blue.

The animal bobbed his head as if he'd heard Sam's silent plea.

"Take me to Luke," she whispered.

Before she lost her courage, she saddled Blue. As an afterthought she grabbed a coil of rope from a hook on the stall door and walked the horse out of the barn. When she attempted to mount, her grip slipped on the saddle horn. She wiped her sweaty palm on her thigh.

A wave of nausea churned Sam's stomach as she adjusted her boot in the stirrup.

She succeeded on the second try, swinging her leg over Blue's rump and settling in the saddle. The horse sidestepped, and bile rose in Sam's throat. When she relaxed her grip on the reins, Blue quieted. "Okay, boy. Take me to Luke."

WADE SLAMMED THE BRAKES on as the car topped the hill near the pond. He held his breath and scanned the water's surface. Nothing. His lungs relaxed and he exhaled. He shifted into Park, left the car and walked the perimeter of the pond, searching for footprints, a dropped fishing pole—any evidence his son had been there. *Nothing.* Certain his son hadn't drowned, Wade headed back to the ranch yard and found Millicent staring into space.

He pulled up next to the old woman and unrolled the window. "Where's the road that leads to the rig?"

"There ain't no road. Ya gotta walk or ride a horse."

He shut off the engine and got out of the car. Riding a horse was out of the question—he'd have to walk. He glanced down at his loafers and cringed. He'd make better time with boots, but it couldn't be helped. "Which way?"

She pointed beyond the barns. "You'll see the nodding donkey once ya clear the hill."

He took off, sprinting the first hundred yards. When his lungs burst into flames he slowed to a trot. As Millicent promised, when he topped the rise he spotted the derrick and Samantha off in the distance.

Where was Luke?

Ignoring the panic building inside him, he squinted into the glare and picked up his pace. The hot sun beat down on his head and sweat poured off his face. As he jogged across the uneven ground his glasses slipped, forcing him to hold them in place. A sharp pain stabbed his side and he sucked in a breath, pushing himself harder.

When he arrived at the well, Samantha was flat on her belly one arm inside a three-foot-wide opening in the ground. "Luke!" he shouted, dropping to his knees.

"Dad?"

Wade nearly wept with relief. "I'm right here, son. Don't move. We'll get you out of there." He stared at Samantha, eyes pleading. "What do we do?" A rescue from an abandoned oil well was out of Wade's area of expertise.

"Get me the rope from the back of Blue's saddle."

Wade stumbled to the horse and fetched the rope, then Samantha made a large loop at the end. "Luke. I'm going to lower a rope into the hole."

"I can't see anything. It's too dark down here."

Closing his eyes, Wade sent up a silent prayer to the heavens.

"You'll have to feel for the rope with your hand. When you find it, put the loop over your head and shoulders, then make sure it's tight around your chest and under your arms," Samantha said.

"Okay."

"How far down is he?" Wade whispered.

"Not too far. Maybe ten feet."

"What's keeping him from falling further down?" Wade made himself ask.

"I'm guessing he landed on a piece of casing that

broke away from the side of the borehole." Samantha lowered the rope into the hole and Wade wrapped the end around his forearm several times.

"Dad?"

"I'm right here, buddy."

"I think my arm's broken. It really hurts."

Wade's heart lodged in his throat. If his son escaped today's catastrophe with a broken arm, Wade would be grateful. "Be brave, Luke. It's going to hurt when we pull you up."

"I got the rope."

"Tell us when you have both arms through the loop and it's tight around your chest."

"I'm ready."

"Use your feet to walk up the hole as we pull you," Samantha instructed.

A thousand worries raced through Wade's mind— Would the rope hold? Would Luke slip out of the loop and fall to his death? Would his son suffer more injuries from being dragged to safety?

Hand over hand, Wade and Samantha reeled Luke up the shaft. Wade heard whimpers and shouted, "Hang on, son, you're almost out!"

When the top of Luke's head popped into view, Wade tightened his grip while Samantha grasped the waist-band of Luke's jeans and hauled him from the hole.

Tears burned Wade's eyes as he hugged his son. "You scared the bejeezus out of us, Luke."

"Ouch, Dad. My arm."

Wade loosened his hold. Luke was a sight to see— covered from head to toe in dirt. His clothes were torn. Scratches marred his face and hands. He looked as if he'd brawled with a pack of wild dogs. "Where are your glasses?"

"They fell off when I slipped into the hole." He sniffed. "I'm in big trouble, aren't I?" Then he looked at Samantha, his tears leaving muddy trails down his cheeks. "I broke your rule, Miss Sam. I'm sorry."

Samantha opened her arms and Luke launched himself at her. "It's okay, honey. I know you didn't mean for this to happen," she whispered. "I'm so glad you're okay."

"We'll discuss your punishment later, Luke. Right now you need to see a doctor." He motioned to the horse. "You can ride back to the barn with Samantha." Wade stood next to the horse, ready to help Samantha and his son mount.

Samantha balked. "I'll walk. Luke should see a doctor as soon as possible."

"I won't risk Luke getting bucked off because I can't ride a horse."

Samantha nodded, then untied the reins from the derrick and mounted. Wade lifted Luke and situated him in front of Samantha.

"My hat, Dad. Where's my hat?"

Wade glanced around and spotted the straw Stetson caught beneath a rusted oil drum. He snatched the hat and placed it on his son's head. "Be careful," he said, then began walking, hoping they wouldn't notice the limp in his stride—his blistered feet hurt like hell.

Samantha clicked her tongue and rode off, Wade following at a distance. He watched until the horse and its riders disappeared over the hill. Left alone he pinched his eyes to stem the flow of tears.

He'd almost lost his son today.

The experience left him gutted. And served as a wake-up call. There was more to life than climbing a damned corporate ladder. He was finished with Dawson Investments. He could only pray Samantha wouldn't be finished with him when he told her his uncle had squandered her trust fund.

AS SOON AS THE BARN CAME into view Sam's body shuddered uncontrollably. When she'd arrived at the oil well and saw the straw cowboy hat lying on the ground, she'd known in her gut that Luke had fallen into the well. On hands and knees she'd searched for the borehole opening and that's when she'd heard Luke's whimper.

God had been watching over Luke, because it was nothing short of a miracle that a piece of casing had prevented him from tumbling several thousand feet to his death.

This accident would have been prevented if she hadn't allowed Wade to persuade her to tackle the ranch improvement projects one at a time instead of all at once as she'd preferred. The first day she took ownership of the ranch she should have hired a construction crew to seal the well and properly cap and bury the wellhead.

Don't blame Wade. You didn't remember to put the oil well on your to-do list.

The paddock blurred before her eyes. Today's catastrophe had destroyed the tiny bead of hope that had been growing inside her since she and Wade had made love. A hope nurtured by her and Wade's deepening relationship and her affection for Luke. A hope that with Wade by her side Sam could have it all—a loving marriage, motherhood and a successful sanctuary ranch.

What a joke. Her life would never be normal. She'd always be a liability to anyone close to her.

Tears dripped off her dirty chin and dropped on Luke's hat.

Wade will forgive you.

The tears leaked faster. Yes, Wade would forgive her, because he was a kind, generous man. He wouldn't just give her one more chance; he'd give her a thousand until her screwups caused a disaster that didn't have today's happy ending.

For Luke's sake, Sam had to say goodbye to Wade.

Chapter Fourteen

Two weeks. Fourteen days. Three hundred and thirty-six hours of pure torture. Wade prayed he hadn't made a mistake avoiding Samantha all this time, while he mapped out the future—a future he hoped she'd share with him.

He merged his BMW onto the highway that would lead to the old Peterson homestead—or Last Chance Ranch as Samantha called it. He glanced in the rearview mirror and cringed at the bags beneath his eyes. Nights of restless sleep and dreams of Samantha telling him to take a hike once she learned of her missing trust fund had taken a toll on him.

Today he intended to make up for his absence. He patted the bump in his trouser pocket—an engagement ring. He'd been tempted to phone Samantha daily—just to hear her voice—but he'd wanted to work out several business details before he dropped to one knee.

Carmen had been his first hurdle. Wade had intended to tell his ex-wife the truth about Luke's mishap at the ranch, but his son had beat him to the punch and lied. After much debate Wade had decided to go along with his son's version of events—Luke had fallen from the top rail of the paddock fence and had landed on his arm.

If Luke had told the truth, Carmen would have forbidden the boy to visit Samantha's ranch. Wade refused to allow his ex-wife to deny their son activities that made him happy—hanging around Samantha and Millicent, and taking care of Blue. Even if Samantha rejected Wade's marriage proposal, he'd suck up his pride and continue to bring Luke to the ranch for riding lessons.

The second hurdle had been his uncle Charles. Wade had informed his uncle that he planned to tell Samantha the truth about her missing funds—only after he'd cleaned out his office and put in his two weeks' notice. Wade had leveled another blow when he'd mentioned Wade's clients would be leaving the firm with him. Charles had been furious, calling Wade an ungrateful bastard. His uncle's reaction and hateful words saddened Wade more than they upset him, freeing the way to leave the company and begin his own investment firm guilt free.

Wade exited the highway and turned onto the gravel road leading to the single-wide trailer. He noted that improvements to the property had ground to a halt since Luke's mishap at the wildcat well. Not that Wade was surprised—Samantha hadn't phoned him asking for more money and when he'd contacted Barney regarding new supply orders the feed store owner claimed Samantha hadn't been in touch with him.

Whisper and an unfamiliar horse grazed in the paddock, but Blue was nowhere in sight when Wade parked his car next to Samantha's truck. He spotted Millicent in her rocker beneath the peach tree. He snatched the gift bag off the passenger seat and called to the old woman. "Morning, Millicent."

"How's Luke's arm healin'?"

"Fine. The red-and-black cast was a hit at school." He held out the bag to her.

"Watcha got there?"

"A gift for you."

She rummaged through the bag. "More chew 'n coffee."

No word of thanks, not even a smile. Wade doubted he'd ever figure out women. He motioned to the trailer. "Samantha around?"

"Yep."

When Millicent didn't elaborate, he prodded, "Where is she?"

"Took Blue out to the fishin' pond." Millicent's wrinkly face puckered like a rotting potato. "That gal's hurtin' real bad."

His chest tightened with worry. "Did she injure herself?"

The question earned him a *whomp* on his thigh.

"Ouch." He rubbed the sore spot. "What did you do that for?"

"'Cause yer a dunderhead."

Dunderhead?

"She's hurtin' here." Millicent patted her heart. "She's afraid ya ain't gonna forgive her fer lettin' Luke wander off."

"I told her it wasn't her fault."

Hadn't he? Wade couldn't remember what he'd said that afternoon. He'd been more concerned with getting Luke to the hospital to have his arm X-rayed.

"The gal's blamin' herself. Ya gotta fix things between ya." Done talking, Millicent gathered her gifts and retreated to her shanty.

Wade hopped into the Beamer and followed the dirt path to the pond. By the time he arrived at the natural spring he swore the car's suspension had been ruined. Samantha gave no indication she'd heard the car. Sitting with her back to Wade, she hugged her knees to her chest and stared into space while Blue grazed nearby.

Where was the strong, determined woman who'd marched into his office demanding her money? Had only mere weeks passed since Samantha Cartwright had blown into his world with the force of an Oklahoma dust storm?

Wade hiked to her spot, pausing a few feet away. He considered a greeting, but they were beyond "Hello's" and "How are you's." He settled on "I've missed you."

Her shoulders rose once, then fell before she rolled to her feet and faced him. The dark smudges beneath her eyes confirmed that she'd been sleeping about as well as he had lately. She inched backward, padding the distance between them.

Don't shut me out. Not when I believe in my heart you're the perfect woman for me.

A breeze kicked up, blowing her hair across her face. She brushed the strands from her eyes—warm pools of brown that he'd drowned in when they'd made love. Finally her gaze landed on his face and his gut clenched at her bleak stare. She opened her mouth to speak, and he feared a "Dear Wade" speech coming his way.

"Wait," he interrupted. "Before you say anything…" If he confessed his love for her first, then she'd believe he was angling for forgiveness when he explained that Dawson Investments had gambled away her trust fund. But if he told her about the missing money first she'd become angry and bitter and refuse to listen to anything more he had to say.

Hell. He was screwed either way.

"No matter how I put this—"

"Then don't, Wade." Samantha knew this time would come. She'd thought she'd be prepared. But there was nothing she could do or say to protect her heart from being broken. Everything inside her yearned for a future with Wade—a chance at their very own fairy-tale life.

She studied Wade's face, committing his features to memory. A strong jaw. Compelling brown eyes that reeled her in with the promise of forgiveness. Another piece of her heart chipped away when he pushed his glasses up the bridge of his nose. When had those stupid black-rimmed specs become so dear?

"There's something I need to tell you." He shoved his hands into his pants pockets.

She steeled herself against the blow she knew was coming, but was unable to dodge. "Go on."

"The real reason I've encouraged you to make repairs to the property one project at a time isn't because I believed it was a better way to manage your money." For the first time since he'd arrived at the pond, Wade didn't make eye contact with her. "My uncle invested your trust fund in a real estate scheme that never panned out."

This didn't sound like an I-never-want-to-see-you-again speech. Confused, she asked, "What are you saying?"

"You're broke, Samantha."

"Broke?" The idea was ludicrous. She was worth millions. "Did you know this before I showed up at your office requesting my money?"

"No. I only found out that afternoon when I accessed your account on the computer."

Her stomach soured. "Why didn't you say something then?"

"At first I'd believed the missing funds had to be caused by a computer glitch. I called in the company's software guru to look into it. After reviewing the computer data he confirmed that the money in your account had been withdrawn but he was unable to locate a tracking number that would tell us where the money went or who took it."

Blinking back tears, she said, "Why didn't you tell me the truth then?" Had the time they spent together meant anything to Wade? Or had he only wanted to keep her distracted while he'd searched for her money?

"I should have been truthful then, but I hadn't been able to get in touch with my uncle." He ran a hand through his hair. "I had hoped to prevent the fiasco from damaging Dawson Investments' reputation and I didn't want this setback to derail the promotion I was up for."

"Why did you need to tell your uncle first?" Wade was in charge of her money not Charles Dawson.

"My uncle was caught on the security tape entering the company offices on July fourth—the day your money was removed from the account."

A gasp worked its way up her throat and exploded from her mouth. "Your uncle stole my money?"

"He used your money to make a bad investment."

Samantha was speechless. It wasn't the shock that Charles Dawson had drained her trust fund dry but the hurt that Wade had tried to protect his uncle and his own interests rather than tell her the truth.

You're one to talk. You've been keeping truths from Wade, as well.

Yes, but…

But nothing. Wade's secret didn't almost cost a little boy his life.

"I'm not proud of myself for misleading you, Samantha."

All this time she'd believed Wade had wanted to be with her because he cared about her not because he'd needed more time to investigate her missing money. Forcing the pain aside she asked, "Where did the money come from for the ranch renovations?"

"I've been using my own cash to finance the repairs and improvements."

How noble.

"By the time I discovered the truth about my uncle's involvement in an investment scheme—"

"What scheme?"

"He invested your money in a real estate deal that went belly-up."

Oh, boy. She wouldn't want to be in Dawson's shoes when her father heard the news.

"According to my uncle it's too late to recoup your losses. He's searching for another investor and if he's able to acquire additional funds, then there's a chance in the end that you'll make a small fortune from this deal."

She couldn't care less if the real estate deal panned out or not. "So digging the well, making calls to suppliers on my behalf and paying the tab at Barney's was to protect you and Dawson Investments?"

"In the beginning, yes," he admitted. "I was in a state of panic and my motives were selfish."

The truth of the matter was that Samantha had been her own worst enemy. She'd gone along with Wade's recommendations because she hadn't been able to trust her memory. The tears she'd held at bay spilled down her cheeks and she swiped angrily at the wetness.

She'd second-guessed herself with every step she'd taken to get the rescue ranch off the ground. Worried and wondered if she was doing the right thing all the while believing Wade had dug that blasted well because he'd wished to please her. More upset with herself than Wade, she lashed out. "You took advantage of me."

"Samantha, I—"

"Stop." Deep down she believed Wade had her best interests at heart. She couldn't blame him for wanting a chance to recover her money. Hadn't she felt the same when she'd bought the Peterson homestead without informing her father, hoping to whip it into shape before she broke the news? "Leave, Wade." When he opened his mouth to protest, she whispered, "Please."

His gaze narrowed and Sam held her breath, wondering if he'd ignore her request. Then he surprised her by closing the gap between them, taking her face in his hands and kissing the daylights out of her.

Shocked by his boldness, Sam froze, her traitorous lips playing along with Wade's.

"You and I aren't finished, Samantha." The pad of his thumb wiped a tear from the corner of her eye. "Not by a long shot."

He drove off, leaving her alone and aching for the impossible—their own happy-ever-after.

"THANK YOU FOR SEEING ME TODAY." Wade stepped into Dominick's downtown Tulsa office. A week had passed since he'd broken the news to Samantha about her trust fund and she'd told him to get lost. He'd returned to his office that day intending to inform her father about her financial losses but the oil baron had been out of town and his secretary hadn't been able to schedule a meeting with Dominick until today.

He'd anticipated a call from Dominick but when none came, Wade assumed Samantha hadn't told her father about the lost millions.

"How's your boy?" Dominick asked.

"Luke's doing great. His broken arm vaulted him to rock-star status among his peers."

Dominick chuckled. "Leave it to kids to turn a near tragedy into an act of heroism." He motioned to the chair in front of his desk. "Have a seat."

"If you don't mind, I'd rather stand."

"In the event you need a quick exit?" One side of Dominick's dark mustache lifted.

"Something like that." Wade shut the office door, then strolled to the bank of windows overlooking the city. He shoved a hand into his trouser pocket and fingered the engagement ring he'd carried around with him each day. "I've already broken the news to Samantha."

"What news?"

Just as he suspected… "I had a hunch Samantha hadn't shared the details with you." Wade braced himself. "What I'm about to disclose will make you madder than hell."

"I'm listening." Dominick set his pen on the desk blotter.

"When Samantha showed up at Dawson Investments on her birthday requesting access to her trust fund, I discovered her account had been wiped clean." To clarify, he added, "The balance was zero." Wade was so damned embarrassed he'd been caught with his shorts down.

Dominick remained silent although his dark eyes glinted. Wade appreciated the man's generosity in allowing him to explain before he raged.

"I suspected a computer glitch. When that assumption proved incorrect, I confronted my uncle." After coming to terms with his uncle's actions, a part of Wade still hungered for the man's recognition and that pissed him off. He acknowledged that letting go of his deep-seated desire for his uncle's approval would take effort on his part. Today's meeting with Dominick was a step in the right direction.

"My uncle invested Samantha's trust fund in a scheme to buy—"

"Son of a bitch." Dominick slammed his fist on his desk. "Charles bought that damned island off the coast of Dubai, didn't he?"

Surprised, Wade asked, "Who told you about the Dubai project?"

"Your uncle urged me to buy in and I refused." He shoved a hand through his hair. "I gave Dawson Investments Samantha's trust fund as a favor to Charles because we went to college together and this is how he repays me?"

Had his uncle stooped so low as to steal Samantha's money because Dominick had refused to invest in a risky real estate venture? Another mark against his uncle—and another reason Wade was glad he'd left the company.

"What happened to the deal?" Dominick asked.

"At the eleventh hour several investors backed out."

"Why didn't Charles follow suit?"

"Samantha's money had already been committed and used to get the project off the ground. The firm is searching for new investors but in all honesty it may be years before Samantha's money is recouped."

"If my daughter's broke who's been funding her pet project?"

"That would be me, sir." Wade loosened the tie around his neck. "I've cashed in my 401(k)."

"That explains the stupid-ass cost-cutting measures." Dominick snorted. "Good God, man. Digging a well by hand?"

Wade's face heated. "That wasn't my brightest moment."

"I'd have to agree." Dominick joined Wade in front of the windows. "I could sue your uncle, bring down his firm and ruin his business reputation."

"You certainly have that right, sir." Wade cleared his throat. "I've left the firm."

"You quit?"

"Yes, sir." He'd spent the past two weeks laying the groundwork to open his own investment firm. He'd wanted the particulars settled before speaking to Samantha again. If she thought he was going to give up on her—them—she didn't know him well. Struggling not to squirm under the older man's scrutiny, Wade said, "I've transferred the remaining money in my 401(k) into a new account for Samantha and I'll continue to build her financial portfolio. If it takes the rest of my life, I'll make sure Samantha is paid back every penny the firm stole from her."

"I'm not going to hold you accountable for your uncle's actions."

"That's generous of you, sir, but I feel obligated to make amends because it happened under my watch." Wade detected a gleam of approval in the old man's eyes.

"You can make amends by opening a new portfolio for my daughter with the money I give you. Then I intend to have a chat with Charles about his business ethics."

Wade would love to be a mouse in his uncle's office when the oil baron dropped by for a visit. "What else is on your mind?" Dominick returned to his desk.

A sudden onset of the shakes drove Wade to sit in a chair. Earlier in the morning he'd rehearsed this speech, but for the life of him he couldn't recall a single argument. "I'm in love with Samantha," he blurted.

Wade had anticipated a slew of reactions from Dominick, none being a blank-face stare. Maybe the old man was hard of hearing. "I said I'm in love with your daughter."

"I heard you the first time." The tap, tap, tap of a pencil eraser against the desk followed the statement.

"I realize this looks bad. If I was in your shoes and a man walked into my office asking permission to marry my daughter after her money had been stolen during his watch I'd wonder if the guy was after my money—of course that's assuming I had your wealth." Wade rubbed a hand down his face. "I'm not saying this very well."

When Dominick didn't come to his rescue, Wade tried again. "I love Samantha. Luke loves her. I can't envision my life without her." He took a deep breath. "I'd like your permission to ask for your daughter's hand in marriage."

"Why?"

Wade frowned. Hadn't he just said why he wanted to marry Samantha?

"Why do you love my daughter?" Dominick repeated.

"What's not to love about her? She's kind and patient with Luke and she has a gentle, giving heart." And Samantha was take-your-breath-away gorgeous.

The man's continued silence unnerved Wade. "I'd also insist on a prenuptial agreement." Wade didn't want Samantha's money—he wanted her. *Damn it, old man, speak.*

"You're not exactly the type of man I envisioned my daughter marrying."

"I'm not much of a cowboy or a roughneck, sir. I can't ride a horse. I don't have experience with cattle, crops or digging oil wells. But—"

"You love my daughter, faults and all," Dominick interrupted.

"No woman is more perfect than Samantha."

Dominick rolled his eyes. "It appears I'm destined not to have a son or son-in-law who appreciates oil as I do. But... You have a healthy respect for money made from my passion for oil. I guess you'll do."

"Then you don't object to me proposing to Samantha?"

"Nope. Give it your best shot, young man."

"Thank you, sir."

Wade paused at the door when Dominick called his name. "Yes, sir?"

"Good luck. You're going to need it."

SAM PARKED HER TRUCK in front of the Lazy River ranch house and took a deep breath. She'd put off this meeting with her father long enough. She didn't relish having to break the news of the loss of her trust fund, but she'd rather discuss money than her failed relationship with Wade.

For the past week Wade had left messages on her cell phone asking to meet with her. The first time he'd called, he'd wanted to take her out to dinner at a swanky restaurant in Tulsa. The second time he'd offered to drop by the ranch during the day. The third time he'd suggested meeting her at the Lazy River. The rest of his messages she'd deleted because listening to his voice had become too painful.

She entered the house through the kitchen door, then padded down the hall to her father's office and rapped her knuckles against the doorjamb.

"It's about time you showed up." He set the paper in his hand aside and motioned her into the room.

"I have something to tell you." Sam took a seat on the leather sofa along the wall.

Her father removed his reading glasses and grinned. "I've been waiting for this news."

What was up with the smile and what *news* was her father referring to? "Wade—"

"Cut to the chase, daughter."

Confused, Sam stared.

"What was your *answer?*"

"Answer to what?" she asked.

He waved a hand before his face. "Never mind. Tell me in your own words."

"Wade informed me that my trust fund has been wiped clean. It's gone. Every last penny of it."

"What else did he have to say?"

"But—"

"Wade already broke the news to me."

Her father's calm demeanor dumbfounded her. "You're not mad? Furious? Irate?"

"I'm more interested in hearing your answer to his question."

Sam had trouble following the conversation. "What question?"

"Good God, daughter. Have you forgotten already?"

Panic raced through Sam as she struggled to recall the details of her talk with Wade at the pond.

"He asked you to marry him, didn't he?"

Her mouth dropped open. *We're not finished, Samantha. Not by a long shot.* But…but… Sam's throat ached so badly she couldn't speak.

"He didn't propose?" The question thundered through the room.

"No." Wade had been calling her to set up a time so he could propose. "He's phoned but I haven't returned his calls." Could it be true? Did Wade really love her? Despite Luke almost… She swallowed hard, unable to finish the thought.

The wall clock ticked off a full minute before her father spoke. "Wade told me about your missing trust fund and then asked for my permission to propose to you."

The tears Samantha had tried to hold at bay the past week dribbled down her cheeks.

"You don't love Wade?" her father asked.

"I love him more than anything, Daddy."

"Then what are you afraid of, honey?"

Be honest. "Myself."

Her father left his chair, sat next to her on the couch and held her hands.

"I love Wade, but I'm afraid I'll slip up and forget a detail that will put him or Luke in danger." She sniffed. "Or make them not love me anymore."

"You're talking crazy, daughter."

"What if Wade and I marry and we have a baby? What if I'm at the mall with the baby and I walk off without the stroller?" She sucked in a ragged breath. "Wade won't be able to trust me with our own children."

"It'll never happen, honey." Her father hugged her. "You know why? Because you'll love your baby and husband so much that your heart won't ever let your brain forget them."

Samantha listened, eager to believe her father's words. "I'm to blame for Luke falling in the well. Wade left him in my care and he almost died."

"That wasn't your fault. The boy disobeyed you and broke the rules."

Was the situation really that straightforward?

"You have so much love to give and—"

"There's a man who desperately wants your love for himself."

Samantha's gaze swung to the doorway where Wade stood.

"I'll start a pot of coffee." Her father left the room.

Lord, she must look a wreck. Samantha wiped her face.

Wade stepped into the room and Sam fought the temptation to launch herself into his arms. "You've been avoiding me, Samantha."

"Yes." She nodded. "I have." *For your own good. And to protect my heart.*

"I'm not going to stop fighting for you. For us and the future I believe we deserve together."

"But—"

"I love you and I don't intend to live my life without you." He took her father's place on the couch, then tucked a strand of hair behind her ear, his fingers trailing across her damp cheek.

"You make my head spin, Samantha. Before I knew what had hit me, you'd crept beneath my defenses one smile…one touch at a time. Then the way you made Luke feel special and important sealed the deal for me."

Wade threaded his fingers through hers. "Most women look at me and see a geek. But in your eyes I'm sexy and desirable." He leaned in and whispered against her ear. "When we made love, I felt like a real cowboy in your arms. Since then all I've ever wanted to do was find a way to sweep you off your feet."

"Oh, Wade…"

"When Luke fell into the well, I realized my priorities were all screwed up. All that I believed important—a promotion at Dawson Investments and my uncle's respect—became meaningless when I faced the possibility of a future without my son and the woman I'd come to love more than life itself." He drew in a deep breath.

"But Luke could have died because of me." She'd been here before—this exact scenario with another man—and the words of reassurance had lasted only a day before he'd changed his mind and hit the road. "And I can't promise that it will never happen again."

She blew out a slow breath and stared Wade in the eye. "You aren't the only one who's kept a secret."

"I doubt it's as bad as—"

She pressed her fingertips against his lips. "I suffered an accident years ago that—"

"Samantha, I know about your memory lapses and trouble concentrating."

"Who told you?"

"My uncle. He said you'd gotten kicked in the head by a horse shortly after our visit to the Lazy River all those years ago."

"Now you understand what a liability I am." Samantha sprang off the couch and paced.

"Luke learned a valuable lesson that day about the consequences of not following rules and listening to adults. Parents aren't perfect. They make mistakes whether they're forgetful or not. In this case, Samantha, you didn't make a mistake—Luke did."

"I'll always pose a risk, Wade. No matter how many notes I write or how hard I concentrate, I'll end up forgetting, which could result in serious consequences."

"If that happens we'll handle it. You're not alone in this, Samantha. You'll have me, Luke, Millicent, your father, friends and family who'll always watch over you." He pulled her into his arms. "What matters most is that your heart never forgets it loves me."

Wade was right. Since he'd entered her life she'd overlooked little things here or there but she'd never forgotten how Wade made her heart sing. How he made her feel complete, whole and perfect.

He caressed her cheek. "You do love me, don't you?"

"With all my heart."

Wade dropped to one knee and clasped her hand. "Samantha. Will you marry me?"

Her own happy-ever-after was really happening. "Yes, Wade. I'll marry you and I promise my heart will never forget how much it loves you at this very moment."

He slipped a simple platinum band with a single solitaire diamond onto her finger, then stood and kissed her until her toes curled. "When I'm old and crotchety I'll become absentminded and you'll have to remind me why I put up with you and that black notebook you carry around."

"You won't get mad when I have to make a note to remind me when to show up at the church for our wedding?"

Wade chuckled. "Not if you don't mind me leaving sticky notes all over the house, requesting your presence in our bedroom."

Sam flashed a sexy smile. "That's one sticky note you'll never have to leave for me. There's no other place I'd rather be than in your arms."

They kissed again—a perfect kiss. One smacking of a new beginning, of burying old fears…of fairy-tale endings.

* * * * *

Be sure to look for Marin Thomas's special holiday collection in December 2009—
two new stories in one!
Available wherever
Harlequin American Romance books are sold.

*Celebrate Harlequin's 60th anniversary with
Harlequin® Superromance®
and the DIAMOND LEGACY miniseries!*

*Follow the stories of four cousins as they come to
terms with the complications of love and what it
means to be a family. Discover with them the
sixty-year-old secret that rocks not one but two
families in...*
A DAUGHTER'S TRUST by Tara Taylor Quinn.

*Available in September 2009 from
Harlequin® Superromance®.*

RICK'S APPOINTMENT with his attorney early Wednesday morning went only moderately better than his meeting with social services the day before. The prognosis wasn't great—but at least his attorney was going to file a motion for DNA testing. Just so Rick could petition to see the child…his sister's baby. The sister he didn't know he had until it was too late.

The rest of what his attorney said had been downhill from there.

Cell phone in hand before he'd even reached his Nitro, Rick punched in the speed dial number he'd programmed the day before.

Maybe foster parent Sue Bookman hadn't received his message. Or had lost his number. Maybe she didn't want to talk to him. At this point he didn't much care what she wanted.

"Hello?" She answered before the first ring was complete. And sounded breathless.

Young and breathless.

"Ms. Bookman?"

"Yes. This is Rick Kraynick, right?"

"Yes, ma'am."

"I recognized your number on caller ID," she said,

her voice uneven, as though she was still engaged in whatever physical activity had her so breathless to begin with. "I'm sorry I didn't get back to you. I've been a little…distracted."

The words came in more disjointed spurts. Was she jogging?

"No problem," he said, when, in fact, he'd spent the better part of the night before watching his phone. And fretting. "Did I get you at a bad time?"

"No worse than usual," she said, adding, "Better than some. So, how can I help?"

God, if only this could be so easy. He'd ask. She'd help. And life could go well. At least for one little person in his family.

It would be a first.

"Mr. Kraynick?"

"Yes. Sorry. I was… Are you sure there isn't a better time to call?"

"I'm bouncing a baby, Mr. Kraynick. It's what I do."

"Is it Carrie?" he asked quickly, his pulse racing.

"How do you know Carrie?" She sounded defensive, which wouldn't do him any good.

"I'm her uncle," he explained, "her mother's— Christy's—older brother, and I know you have her."

"I can neither confirm nor deny your allegations, Mr. Kraynick. Please call social services." She rattled off the number.

"Wait!" he said, unable to hide his urgency. "Please," he said more calmly. "Just hear me out."

"How did you find me?"

"A friend of Christy's."

"I'm sorry I can't help you, Mr. Kraynick," she said softly. "This conversation is over."

"I grew up in foster care," he said, as though that gave him some special privilege. Some insider's edge.

"Then you know you shouldn't be calling me at all."

"Yes… But Carrie is my niece," he said. "I need to see her. To know that she's okay."

"You'll have to go through social services to arrange that."

"I'm sure you know it's not as easy as it sounds. I'm a single man with no real ties and I've no intention of petitioning for custody. They aren't real eager to give me the time of day. I never even knew Carrie's mother. For all intents and purposes, our mother didn't raise either one of us. All I have going for me is half a set of genes. My lawyer's on it, but it could be weeks—months—before this is sorted out. Carrie could be adopted by then. Which would be fine, great for her, but then I'd have lost my chance. I don't want to take her. I won't hurt her. I just have to see her."

"I'm sorry, Mr. Kraynick, but…"

* * * * *

Find out if Rick Kraynick will ever have a chance to meet his niece.
Look for A DAUGHTER'S TRUST
by Tara Taylor Quinn,
available in September 2009.

Copyright © 2009 by Tara Taylor Quinn

We'll be spotlighting a different series
every month throughout 2009
to celebrate our 60th anniversary.

**Look for Harlequin® Superromance®
in September!**

*Celebrate with
The Diamond Legacy
miniseries!*

Follow the stories of four cousins as they come to terms
with the complications of love and what it means to
be a family. Discover with them the sixty-year-old secret
that rocks not one but two families.

A DAUGHTER'S TRUST by *Tara Taylor Quinn*
September

FOR THE LOVE OF FAMILY by *Kathleen O'Brien*
October

LIKE FATHER, LIKE SON by *Karina Bliss*
November

A MOTHER'S SECRET by *Janice Kay Johnson*
December

Available wherever books are sold.

www.eHarlequin.com

HSRBPA09

You're invited to join our Tell Harlequin Reader Panel!

By joining our new reader panel you will:

- Receive Harlequin® books—they are FREE and yours to keep with no obligation to purchase anything!
- Participate in fun online surveys
- Exchange opinions and ideas with women just like you
- Have a say in our new book ideas and help us publish the best in women's fiction

In addition, you will have a chance to win great prizes and receive special gifts! See Web site for details. Some conditions apply. Space is limited.

To join, visit us at
www.TellHarlequin.com.

THBPA0108

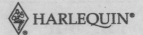

HARLEQUIN®

American ★ Romance®

The Ranger's Secret
REBECCA WINTERS

When Yosemite Park ranger Chase Jarvis rescues
an injured passenger from a downed helicopter,
he is stunned to discover it's the woman he
once loved. But Chase is no longer the man
Annie Bower knew. Will she forgive him for
the secret he's been keeping for ten long years?
And will he forgive Annie for her own secret—
the daughter Chase didn't know he had…?

*Available September
wherever books are sold.*

"LOVE, HOME & HAPPINESS"

www.eHarlequin.com

HAR75279

Stay up-to-date on all your romance reading news!

The Harlequin Inside Romance newsletter is a **FREE** quarterly newsletter highlighting our upcoming series releases and promotions!

Go to
eHarlequin.com/InsideRomance
or e-mail us at
InsideRomance@Harlequin.com
to sign up to receive
your **FREE** newsletter today!

You can also subscribe by writing to us at: HARLEQUIN BOOKS
Attention: Customer Service Department
P.O. Box 9057, Buffalo, NY 14269-9057

Please allow 4-6 weeks for delivery of the first issue by mail.

IRNBPAQ209

REQUEST YOUR FREE BOOKS!
2 FREE NOVELS PLUS 2
FREE GIFTS!

American ★ Romance®

Love, Home & Happiness!

YES! Please send me 2 FREE Harlequin® American Romance® novels and my 2 FREE gifts (gifts are worth about $10). After receiving them, if I don't wish to receive any more books, I can return the shipping statement marked "cancel." If I don't cancel, I will receive 4 brand-new novels every month and be billed just $4.24 per book in the U.S. or $4.99 per book in Canada.* That's a savings of close to 15% off the cover price! It's quite a bargain! Shipping and handling is just 50¢ per book. I understand that accepting the 2 free books and gifts places me under no obligation to buy anything. I can always return a shipment and cancel at any time. Even if I never buy another book from Harlequin, the two free books and gifts are mine to keep forever.

154 HDN EYSE   354 HDN EYSQ

Name	(PLEASE PRINT)	
Address		Apt. #
City	State/Prov.	Zip/Postal Code

Signature (if under 18, a parent or guardian must sign)

Mail to the **Harlequin Reader Service:**
IN U.S.A.: P.O. Box 1867, Buffalo, NY 14240-1867
IN CANADA: P.O. Box 609, Fort Erie, Ontario L2A 5X3

Not valid to current subscribers of Harlequin® American Romance® books.

Want to try two free books from another line?
Call 1-800-873-8635 or visit www.morefreebooks.com.

* Terms and prices subject to change without notice. Prices do not include applicable taxes. N.Y. residents add applicable sales tax. Canadian residents will be charged applicable provincial taxes and GST. Offer not valid in Quebec. This offer is limited to one order per household. All orders subject to approval. Credit or debit balances in a customer's account(s) may be offset by any other outstanding balance owed by or to the customer. Please allow 4 to 6 weeks for delivery. Offer available while quantities last.

Your Privacy: Harlequin is committed to protecting your privacy. Our Privacy Policy is available online at www.eHarlequin.com or upon request from the Reader Service. From time to time we make our lists of customers available to reputable third parties who may have a product or service of interest to you. If you would prefer we not share your name and address, please check here. ☐

HAR09R

In 2009 Harlequin celebrates
60 years of pure reading pleasure!

We're marking this occasion by offering
16 **FREE** full books to download and read.

Visit

www.HarlequinCelebrates.com

to choose from a variety of
great romance stories
that are absolutely **FREE!**

(Total approximate retail value of $60)

We invite you to visit and share the Web site
with your friends, family
and anyone who enjoys reading.

SMP60WEB1

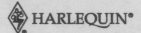

HARLEQUIN®

American ★ Romance®

COMING NEXT MONTH
Available September 8, 2009

#1273 DOCTOR DADDY by Jacqueline Diamond
Men Made in America
Dr. Jane McKay wants a child more than anything, but her dreams
of parenthood don't include the sexy, maddening doctor next door.
Luke Van Dam is *not* ready to settle down. Yet the gorgeous babe magnet
seems to attract *babies*, too—he's just become guardian of an infant girl.
Is Luke the right man to share Jane's dream after all?

#1274 ONCE A COP by Lisa Childs
Citizen's Police Academy
Roberta "Robbie" Meyers wants a promotion out of the Lakewood P.D. vice
squad so she can spend more time with her daughter. Holden Thomas sees only a
woman with a job that's too dangerous for a mother. So the bachelor guardian
strikes Robbie off his list of mommy candidates for the little girl under his care.
Too bad he can't resist the attractive cop's charms!

#1275 THE RANGER'S SECRET by Rebecca Winters
When Chase Jarvis rescues an injured passenger from a downed helicopter, the
Yosemite ranger is stunned to discover it's the woman he once loved. But he is
no longer the man Annie Bower knew. Will she forgive him for the secret he's
been keeping for ten long years? And will he forgive Annie her own secret—the
daughter Chase didn't know he had…?

#1276 A WEDDING FOR BABY by Laura Marie Altom
Baby Boom
Gabby Craig's pregnancy is a dream come true. Too bad the father is an
unreliable, no-good charmer who's left town. And when his brother, Dane, steps
in to help, Gabby can't help relying on the handsome, *responsible* judge. But
how can she be falling for the brother of her baby's daddy?

www.eHarlequin.com

HARCNMBPA0809